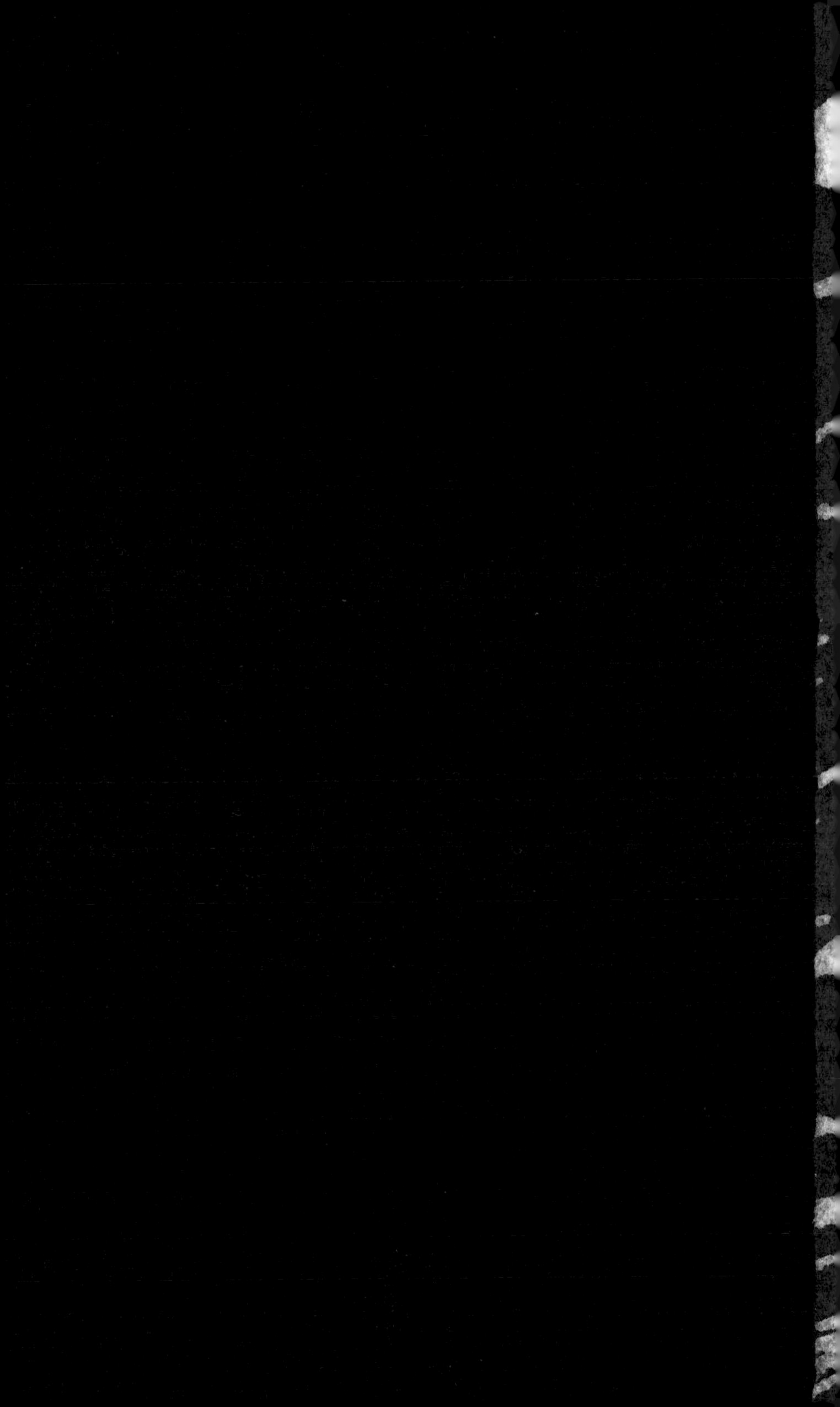

I'll Be Watching

I'LL BE WATCHING

,,,,,,

PAMELA PORTER

GROUNDWOOD BOOKS
HOUSE OF ANANSI PRESS
TORONTO BERKELEY

Published in Canada and the USA in 2011 by Groundwood Books

Groundwood Books / House of Anansi Press
110 Spadina Avenue, Suite 801, Toronto, Ontario M5V 2K4
or c/o Publishers Group West
1700 Fourth Street, Berkeley, CA 94710

We acknowledge for their financial support of our publishing program the Canada Council for the Arts, the Government of Canada through the Canada Book Fund (CBF) and the Ontario Arts Council.

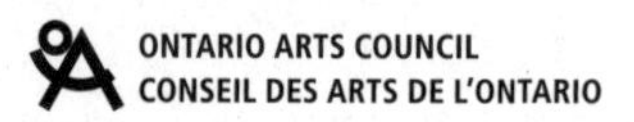

Library and Archives Canada Cataloguing in Publication

Porter, Pamela Paige
I'll be watching / Pamela Porter.

ISBN 978-1-55498-095-6 (bound).—ISBN 978-1-55498-096-3 (pbk.)

I. Title.

PS8581.O7573I55 2011 jC813'.6 C2011-900509-3

Cover art by Murray Kimber
Design by Michael Solomon

Groundwood Books is committed to protecting our natural environment. As part of our efforts, this book is printed on paper that contains 100% post-consumer recycled fibers, is acid-free and is processed chlorine-free.

Printed and bound in Canada

For Rob, Cecilia and Drew.
I love you dearly
and forever.

And for Marilyn
in memory of her father,
Edgar Pinder,
youngest of the four.

I'll Be Watching

Prologue

I should have come back
before they burned down the elevator,
before the train slouched off to die,
before the last stubborn citizen was laid to rest in the cemetery.

At Bob Lively's corner station
the pumps wait like one-armed bald men
rusting in dry grass, cursed and turned to steel.
Now the only thing that tells you you're in
Argue, Saskatchewan,
is the shadow of paint on the forehead of the Mercantile.

I'd forgotten how the wind here is always in your face.
I remembered the school facing north, not east.
What happened to the shouting at recess? If I glance
from the corner of my eye, will I see us there —
swing and a miss,
another swing and crack of the bat, an explosion of dust,
and Miss Parker overseeing us all?

And when did our house blow away like dust?
I stand at the spot where it used to weather our storms;
I try in my mind to place the furniture on this patch of ground
where we grew like weeds and doubted
we were strong enough for the world.

How to tell Nora it's gone —
our screen door warped like a shell,

the little rooms where we snuffed the flickering lamplight
and slept beneath the eye of the moon.
The railroad track a rack of weathered bones
                                        from here to the horizon,
this poor stretch of earth that was all the world to us.

Nora says, *Jim, we know it happened.*
Nobody can tell us it didn't happen.
Not as long as we still remember.

October 1941

I

The Children

Nora Loney

We're hardly through the second month of school
and Jim's declaring he'll quit.
How can he quit school
when he's twelve years old?
Does he think he'll get a job?
He ought to know better.
He watched Ran walk out on school at fifteen,
and it took till he was sixteen to get but three days a week
with the railroad.
Except for harvest, Ran spends the rest of his time
just like every other man in town with nothing to do:
standing around the stove at the Argue Mercantile
or laying down a thin dime for coffee at the New Moon,
or, when he's broke, shooting the breeze
with Danny Filmore down at the telegraph office.

It was the argument about Pluto yesterday
got Jim tied in a knot over school. Mr. Lahr
claimed he's never heard of Pluto, declared
we've got eight planets in our solar system,
no more. Jim fired back, saying Pluto
was discovered exactly eleven years ago *for crying out loud.*
Well, my genius brother got a grim smile from Mr. Lahr
and two strikes on his open palms with the cane,
and so Jim sat in a pool of rage the rest of the day.

Today he's decided he'd rather speed ahead of us
than shuffle along behind

with his aching hands shoved into his pockets.
Those ears of his must be burning without his tuque.

Tonight is Parent Night at school.
After lunch we'll decorate the room
and practice our speeches and songs and what have you.
I do hope Papa at least will attend.
Oh, what am I saying?
Addie — *Come.*

Margaret Loney (deceased)

My darling Nora, already fourteen years old —
I can hardly believe it!
You're dashing out the door for school,
dragging Addie by the hand, Jim dawdling as usual,
now racing ahead of you both, and Jim's
gone and left his tuque. Again.
It won't help matters a bit that he'll remember
once the wind turns his ears to fire.
He'll tell himself he doesn't need it.

You don't know how helpless I feel, that boy
always going off without one thing or another.
You remember, don't you, darling,
how I'd rush out behind you three, not even
taking time to close the door? I think I
embarrassed Jim half to death with my shrill
call down the road, some sweater or mitten
or lunch flapping from the clothesline end of my arm.

Winter's surely a-comin' in —
as your grandfather used to say — that fearsome

chill that cuts right through. Especially me,
as you can imagine, dear, in my present condition.

Ever dependable, my only, my beautiful daughter,
tugging at Addie's hand, passing these burned-black fields
is enough to make a person believe there's no loveliness
left on earth.
I want you to hear me, what with all that's coming.

First of all, a young lady needs a good haircut.
Go to Esther. She'll charge fifty cents, but it's worth it.
A good cut makes all the difference. Now.
A mother tries her level best to love her children the same,
but she can't help having favorites.
It's that special one, the child
you don't know will be right in the end, the one
who's been touched.
Hold onto our Addie.
Don't let anyone pry him away from you.

Our Jim now, he'll be a fine man, a sensible
head on his shoulders when push comes to shove,
and how he's stretching up so tall! I do believe
he's nearly as tall as I was.
Don't let that quitting school business get to you.
It will blow over soon enough. He'll be well, Jim will.

But Randall, my eldest — the only apple
of my eye for his first two years — I have to confess
I *am* worried. There's a war to be fought
and he's of fighting age, or nearly. He's not above lying
about his years. How do you think he got that job
with the railroad?
He'll pass, too, tall as he is,
disgruntled, restless.

I'm sorry, darling. This isn't what I wanted.
I wished better for you than this.
A crinoline dress. Silk sash.
When I find you sleeping,
I take that little piece of your hair and tuck it back,
just the way I used to.
You know I'd take your burden if I could.

Now, about your father.
Try not to lay blame. Try to ignore the talk.
It was too much for him — the trenches, the rats,
the way death stuck to him like mud.
He was so young.
The man who returned to marry me was not the boy
who left and for whom I waited and prayed every night,
Dear Jesus, return him to me whole.

Darling, what happened to me was not entirely his fault.
The roads were slick,
and those blasted ditches on either side!
I thank the good Lord every day it was I
flew through that windshield,
not any of you. I'm grateful to the blessed Jesus
that you were piled asleep back there like a litter of kittens,
that Ran stayed home.

Nora, you're the strongest of all of us.
Somewhere inside, you know it.
When you come through the door this afternoon
and stumble upon Jim's tuque just here —
on the floor —

think that it was I looking after you.

Jim Loney

What's the point of school when the teacher knows nothing?
Pluto is a fact.
Discovered by Clyde Tombaugh, amateur astronomer
at Lowell Observatory, Flagstaff, Arizona, 1930.
In eleven years, word should have gotten around.

I'd quit school except I'd miss
playing war games with Frank.
We've carved our own planes from sticks,
keep them in our cigar box hangar, take them out
at lunch and recess
while Addie circles us, hopping up and down
and waving his little hands in the air.

We haven't heard a word out of Addie's mouth
since Mama died.
At first no one noticed, but now it's getting creepy.
He can sneak up on a person like a ghost.
Old man Lahr sure doesn't like the sound
of a kid who doesn't talk.
He said, "You think that's why I'm here?
So you can fiddle with your fingers?
SIT ON THOSE HANDS."
And Addie sat on his hands until he had to scratch his nose.
Lahr snuck up from behind and whapped him
with the cane, right on the top of Addie's head.
That got a jump out of Addie, but no sound.
Nora found him later, curled up in the cloakroom
under a pile of coats.
Dried his face and took him home.

That was the first and only time Papa set foot
inside the school. I figure Papa had to get pretty buttered up

with Elmer Spanner's rye whiskey
to go cuss out the teacher.

If I told Pap Lahr caned me,
he'd just say I deserved it.

Carol Williams, Postmistress

I run the post office here in Argue.
My father held the office of postmaster before me.
He wanted to pass this job onto his son,
if he ever got one. Had five daughters,
and I'm the eldest.
Everybody in town comes in here.
I mean *everybody*. My post office
is right at the back of the Mercantile.
Through my window I see and hear it all.
Every evening when I close up,
I see Freeman helping George Loney home.

That Nora now. Nice girl, polite,
always leading little Addie by the hand
as if she was his mother.
Those children.
Nearly everybody's poor here — dust got us all.
You do have some exceptions, of course.
And in the midst of it, their mother up and dies.
Automobile accident. Blizzard. It didn't help
that George was driving. They say
he had liquor on his breath, but who really knows?
People can say whatever they like and make it true
just by getting someone else to repeat it.

Terrible for those children.
And George hasn't taken it well atall.

Well, Mrs. Effie Slade, see, she had a son,
handsome little boy. He took fever and then
turned out it was that infantile paralysis.
Went into his chest
and that precious little boy died. Three years old.
That was back in '37. A bad year for the polio. Mmmmm.

After his boy passed on, Stanley Slade
took off for Alberta. Wasn't much to keep him here,
and I guess what was left of the two of them, him
and Effie, died too with that little fellow.

A few of the women got bees in their bonnets
and decided Effie needed some children to take care of,
and lo and behold here were four of 'em
right in town and motherless to boot.

Well, she hasn't taken to them well atall.
Nice enough children, but some say
the Lord took their mother away for a reason.

Personally, I don't see how a person can blame children.
Suffer the little children to come unto me, our Lord said.

Now, little Addie, he had a sickness himself once,
and it seems to have affected some part of his brain.
He is a bit touched, you see. I myself have never
heard that child talk.

Effie now. She's got a row to hoe,
taking on four children and a husband who,
well, has a liking for the bottle,
if you know what I mean.

George Loney

We were lucky to get this house. We were.
Not a lot of people come and go from Argue.
Other folks walked off their farms,
                    struck out from here to Vancouver
looking for a place to live, work to do.
I got this job with the railroad,
                    and there was an empty house in town,
once used for storing grain.
I helped my Maggie sweep it out, and yes,
sometimes grain still falls out of the cupboards
but it's a good solid house.

This house isn't crowded up with a bunch
                    of other houses around it — no,
there's wheat fields just out the kitchen window.
I thought my Maggie would like that.
She loved the farm.

Gawdammit, I didn't want to sell,
give up, let go of Ike and Nell.
They just looked at me with their wet eyes
and asked me why. Horses talk.
They put that thought in my head: *why*.

I knew it was my fault.
Every day now, I knock off work,
just want to get that gawdam roof off my head.
Used to be out in the open air all the time.

Elmer Spanner — runs the Buffalo Bar — he says,
"Look, George, I tell ya and I tell ya.
                              It wasn't your fault.
Gawdam government's fault. It's the *truth*, George Loney.

"Nobody, and I mean *nobody* in Ottawa cares
about us wretched suckers out here on the prairie.
We grow their food.
Then what do they do?
They claim it comes from a gawdam store.
That's how come they don't notice if we starve out here."

And now my Maggie's gone.
I'll tell the truth —
I had no liquor that night. It was snow
and a howling wind. Tossed that car
like it was a child's toy.
When they found us, I was drunk on grief and rage.

Maggie would never approve of me marrying Effie.
Summer coming, the kids running around,
nobody to tell 'em eat, sleep, brush your teeth.

I don't know how to gawdam cook.
I don't know how to gawdam cook.

I don't know how to help Nora with that woman stuff.

I try to keep the kids fed and clothed. And I try to forget.

Everybody thinks Maggie's dead and gone.
But she ain't dead in me. Every day
I hear her talking. *George Loney,*
she says. *George, now look what you've gone and done.*
And I loved you for this?

That's why I try to forget.
But my Maggie, she won't let me.

Margaret Loney

I just want you children to know
I'm not speaking to your father right now.
I've given up standing beside his bed at night,
waking him with my disapproval.
I've stopped picking up his towel and socks
so *she* doesn't dress him down
for leaving them on the floor.
Marrying a woman he doesn't love
and letting her sleep on *my* side of the bed —
I can't stand it any longer.

I knew the farm would break him
before it broke me. I knew it before I married him.
In the end, the farm broke us all.
The end of the farm was just the beginning —
having to move into town,
this little Eaton's Catalogue house,
hardly bigger than your thumb.
In those days the bank took the farms
and let the people wither.

I could see plain as a cloudless day
the farm had broken *his* father.
And George was set to inherit it.
The summer I was sixteen,
I was passing the Loney farm at harvest —
two teams of horses hitched to the harvester —
that big belt and clackety engine
making all the noise in the world.

But George, he ran over to me, his gloves
clasped like a bouquet of flowers in his hand,
and he tipped his hat, grinning ear to ear.

I loved him right then and there.

That autumn, 1916, he left with all the other
fresh-faced farm boys for the war in Europe.

In two years I received twenty-six letters and knew
at least, until the date of each,
George was alive.
When I saw him again,
I knew by his face in the train window
George Loney was changed.

I married the boy, but I got the man.

Effie Slade

The Lord giveth, and the Lord taketh away.
I've taken away that boy's tuque, stuffed it
under my bed, so he can't find it
even if he wants it.
I've had it up to *here*
picking up after those children.
But then, look at their father. You know what they say,
The apple never falls far from the tree.
Lost what land was left to him,
and finally lost the whole farm.
Lots of people got their farms foreclosed,
but I say the Lord has smote these people for a reason.

I used to have my own life. My own child. I blame
Stanley Slade for dropping my mother's umbrella
inside the front door of our house. Mother
had foreseen my brother's death

when that very umbrella slipped
from her hand, and she knew. Even before
the telegram arrived from Flanders.

I saw the umbrella, black as death, falling
out of Stanley's hand and knew it was some terrible
bad luck. Means there will be a murder in the family.
Mother always said so, and she was right.

Wasn't two weeks after, our boy took ill
and Stanley Slade delayed bringing the doctor in.
He would've charged a dollar and Stanley
said we didn't have a dollar.
I say he killed my boy.

And now what have I got? George Loney is what I got.
And four kids that don't belong to me.
One with a little bitty job that pays a widow's mite
and one that goes around
                    drawing pictures in the air
and won't look you in the eye.

Any child won't look you in the eye
            has got malice on his mind.
Everybody in town looks at him and wonders
what is wrong with that child.

            I say it'd be better for us all
if someone took him to Weyburn
and dropped him off.

Carol Williams

Like I say, I see everybody in here.
Ethel Meany come in for her mail, said, did I see
in the *Moose Jaw Herald*
that Winnipeg is having blackout drills?
They're making every single person in the entire city
cover their windows at night.
"Now, that's just good sense,"
Ethel says. "With all those big airplanes nowadays,
the Germans could just fly over here one night
and bomb us all to smithereens." Ethel says
she read those airplanes can cross the ocean
like it's an itty-bitty lake.

Then Louise Gillingham pipes up,
"Now why don't we do that?
More and more little towns like us have got power now,
and we're just a bunch of shining little targets.
Why, Hitler's goons could be flying over,
looking for Winnipeg and miss it, being blacked out,
and they'd mistake us for them.
It could happen, you know."

Then Ethel says she heard Geraldine McHattie
at church circle say *she* heard on the radio
how Germans have been sneaking over to Canada
to spy on us.
Radio said it doesn't matter
if they've been your neighbors for years,
or if they come over a long time ago or anything like that.
They've just been biding their sweet time
till Hitler took over.

And I said, "Honestly, can you believe anything

Geraldine says?
Why, she came home from Regina last week
with the worst manicure I have ever seen on a living person."

Personally, I do my nails myself.
People always notice the little things.

Franz Lahr, Schoolteacher

I say to these children, "These are the best years of your lives.
You have someone to cook and clean up after you
and wash your clothes, and all you have to do
is go to school."

I have ten grades to teach. Forty-four children in all.
This town — how shall I put it — the welcome
I initially received has dried up
like a leaf in winter.

Things might have turned out differently
had the war not kicked up in Europe. No Hitler,
no rumors in the newspapers of German spies
hiding on the prairies.

Now anyone with a German name is suspect.
If your horse has a German name, better change it,
or the owner is suspect.

Just a month ago, two RCMP officers came to town
to pay me a little visit.
Asked strange questions,
walked through this cramped teacherage
looking for secret closets, trap doors in the floor.

Well, it surprised them
how a small-town schoolteacher lives.
This house — if you can call two rooms
and a tacked-on lavatory a house —
has no closets at all.
All my clothes, my books, my cooking spoons
are lying in plain sight.

Even if I wanted to be a spy, what would I report?
That Louise Gillingham's chickens broke loose last Wednesday?
Every time I go out my front door, someone's watching me.
What else have they got to do?
When I take Mary-Ann Meany walking on a country road,
everyone knows what time we went out,
and they speculate on what we will say and do.

What they don't know is
we talk about Blake. Yes, Blake.
I've found one person in this town
who has actually heard of William Blake.
We walk the roads out of town
and read Blake to each other.
And here's a little secret:
Mary-Ann fancies herself a poet.
Now and again she'll bring me a poem she's written
after one of our Blake walks.
I've not tried to discourage her,
though probably I should.

Last night,
Mary-Ann shoved her hand in mine.
I held it nervously. I supposed she could feel
sweat dampening our hands. Finally, she asked me
why don't I kiss her?
We stood there in the failing light of autumn,

two strands of her hair blowing across her pretty face.
What could I tell her? That I don't know
if I have it in me, the urges other men
feel for a woman? What
would happen to me if I said that?

I spend my days with forty-four unruly creatures,
including that Addie Loney who won't talk
and probably belongs at the Mental over in Weyburn,
and I spend my evenings walking with Mary-Ann,
or sitting alone in my mouse-hole house,
listening to the night winds,
the muttering of the roadside weeds.

Jim Loney

As soon as Lahr lets us out for the day, me and Frank
go back to our war game. We have our spot
behind the school — out of Papa's way.
I've learned not to have friends over to our house
once the Buffalo closes for dinner hour.

Papa never has much to say till he's been to the bar.
Then he'll stumble home singing, *Holy, Holy, Holy,*
Lord Gawd Almighty…
even though he hasn't been inside a church
since Mama died.

Once Papa gets near, he'll slap Frank
on the back and say, *What a handsome lad!*
Why, my best friend,
Harrison Davies,
had your dark hair, same blue eyes. Know

what happened to Harrison? Seventeen years old.

Then Papa goes quiet. Can hardly hear him.
Starts walking away —
Gawdam lungs burned out,
gangrene in both his feet.
Buried him at Passchendaele.

Then Papa will shuffle home to his chair by the radio
and he'll slide back into his silence
and just when you're thinking you won't hear
another word out of his mouth till Christmas,
he'll look up at one of us and say, *Well,*
aren't you having a nice childhood?

I see Papa coming, his face shining
like a bank clock,
Gideon Freeman leading him home, I know
it's past five.
I tell Frank, *Your mum's calling you to supper.*

Frank Selemka

Jim Loney's my best friend.
We got a collection of war planes
we made from sticks and our pocket knives —
four Hurricanes, a Halifax,
three Spitfires, a Beaufort bomber
and a German Messerschmitt.
We take turns
holding the Mess in the air,
then we swarm it with the Allied planes.

First, the Mess sends a couple of our Hurricanes
spiraling into the ground
trailing smoke and flames.
Addie makes the smoke by kicking up dirt with his shoe.

Then we fire back with the Halifax and Beaufort.
Flak flies. Hits the Mess.
All the hundreds of Messes
we imagine flying around us.
Then the Spitfire comes out —
Hilly Brown, RAF fighter pilot, takes care of the rest.

I listen to the news on our radio every night
so I know what our planes have to do the next day.

We've bombed the *Bismarck* about a million times.
We've gained ground knocking the Krauts out of France.

Until his pa comes home. Then Jim says,
Your mum's calling you to supper.

That's how he tells me he's got to go.
That's just his way.

Nora Loney

Mr. Lahr kept us overtime
because of the older boys' antics.
Whenever they exasperate him, Lahr
throws down his eraser cloth and a little cloud
of chalk dust sprays his shoes.
"If you ruffians cannot respect
the value of an *ed-u-ca-tion*,"

he boomed, "I'm sure the fellas at the enlistment office
would be more than happy
to use you as cannon fodder."

When he finally let us go, Jim and Frank rushed out
like a gale-force wind.
I gathered my books.

In the schoolyard three of the boys circled
around Addie.
Others gathered around to watch.

That big oaf Red O'Callahan held a cocked
mouse trap in his palm, saying,
"Get the cheese!"
I grabbed Addie's raised hand and tugged him
out of the circle.

Rushing through the front door of our house,
I saw Effie standing in the hallway
with her face set to give a sermon.
"Twelve minutes late.
What did I tell you to do about your tardiness, young lady?"

"You told me to pray about it," I said.

"Obviously, you didn't do it. You don't listen
to a word I say, do you? No.
If your mother had taught you little heathen to pray,
I wouldn't be in this mess. Well, just remember this,
Little Miss:
'For he who doest not the will of God
will be thrown into the fire.'"

Effie can quote scripture better than the preacher.

I spotted Jim's tuque on the floor
just behind the door,
bent down to snatch it up. Effie
stared at that tuque like she'd seen a ghost.

Once Papa came through the door, Effie
rebuked him for the whiskey on his breath,
and started on about Noah, how after
he let all the animals off the ark,
Noah got drunk.
You have to read it in the Bible yourself.
They never teach it to you in Sunday School.

Papa strode past her, shouting, "Good God, woman!
Don't go hurling invectives!"
And he went straight for his chair, turning it
so it faced the corner, where he sat, silent.

Effie clenched her teeth.
"I didn't hurl a thing at you, buster."
Papa laced his hands over his chest like he
was playing dead. She stood over him.
"And some people in town claim
I married you for your money. Ha!"

Addie, with his impeccable timing,
chose that moment to present each of them
invitations to Parent Night.

Effie said, "What are you giving me
an invitation for? I'm not your mother."

Papa turned around in his chair, said, "Well,
aren't you having a nice childhood —
making paper pretties at school. When I was your age

I was driving a team o' horses already."

I wanted desperately for Papa to come.

I dreaded with my whole heart
that Papa might come.

Margaret Loney

To quiet them all, Nora
put a basket in Addie's hand,
ushered him out the door
          and toward the hen house.

I followed my Addie out,
felt something in my thinness
like a shudder.
Addie tossed out grain
just as he'd been shown,
then slipped into the coop to gather eggs.

I saw the eye, the snout
beneath that place in the floor
where the knot of wood had fallen out.
I felt the loose plank rise, and sudden,
the weasel — in the eggs,
his smoke-brown face smeared
with yolk, white and bits of shell.

Addie, I tried, honey, I tried,
but when you ran,
the toe of your shoe
where the stitching had come undone

caught on the step, and you flew flat
onto the shallow basket
you'd gathered them into.

It was all Nora could do
to save half a dozen, take you
by the hand, wipe the tears
you made without sound
but for your shaken breathing,
wipe your hands, leave your clothes
in the sink and dress you clean.

That woman never turned her head to notice.

Ran Loney

I came up the front steps right after Jim,
always try to plan my entrance so dinner
will be waiting on the table.

Through the front window I could see them all:
Jim hanging up his jacket, Nora in the kitchen
kneeling in front of Addie, Pop in his chair
and Effie arched over him —
like characters in a play without sound.

Some nights I'm on the rail
from here to Moose Jaw and back.
I even get my own bed. Nothing fancy, mind you,
but it's mine.
At home there's one lousy bed for three boys.
There is no torture in the world to compare
with the feeling of two heavy, sweaty, snoring bodies

lying on top of you.

Last night I sat with Howard Selemka,
one of a groundswell of small-town guys
just a year or two older than me,
                heading to RCAF training
and acting like they got a free ticket to see the world.

When I wasn't walking the aisles
          selling peanuts and playing cards,
I showed Howard my cot. He was looking forward
to having his own bed at training school.
Freedom from the curse of the sagging mattress
and sweaty brothers.

Those nights I eat in the dining car
after all the passengers have gone back to their seats.
It's peaceful to look out the window
          at every field and slough,
abandoned farmhouses leaning away from the wind,
doors and windows like two eyes and a mouth
that can't figure out what the hell happened.

Working the train's a lonely life,
                    a sweet loneliness,
the way reflections in the windows at night
give you the feeling the train is full of spirits,
as if the present is just layered over the past.

When I burst into our house, Pop was facing the wall,
his cracked hands clasped over his chest,
doing his damndest to ignore Effie.
I slipped Addie a lemon drop from my pocket.

Over fried eggs — what were left, anyway, from the disaster —

and potatoes and bread with butter,
Pop grunted when asked if he'd come to Parent Night.
Jim could barely curl his swollen fingers around his fork.
I recognized the marks.
I left school the day Lahr did that to me,
decided it was for the last time and made good on my promise.

I said, "So little Hitler is having the parents in?"

Effie said, "Someone should make him
shave off that moustache.
It's a sin to want to look like the devil himself.
If he won't try to be like the rest of us
he oughta be run out of town on a rail."

"Well, I'm going," I said.
Everybody looked up at me. "To Parent Night, that is.
Nothing else to do in this God-forsaken town."

Nora glared at me.
Addie got so excited
he started flapping his hands in the air.
How he makes such elaborate designs with his fingers
is a puzzle to me.

Jim Loney

Our school was lit up like church
and it looked like everyone in town was headed there.
Papa and Ran came with us. Effie
was home listening to *The Gospel Hour*
on the radio. She never misses it.
At the steps to the school, Papa took out his watch,

said, "Be right in. Save me a seat."

Ran sat in the back row and tilted his chair against the wall.
King George stared down from the wall
with the same grim face he wore every day.

The youngest went first, except Addie, of course.
Just before me was Frank, who recited a speech
about Alexander Graham Bell and the telephone.

I kept looking around for Papa to show up,
but then Mr. Lahr announced I'd be reciting the poem,
"Joy and Woe," by Mr. William Blake,

so I stood at the front of the room, cleared my voice
and began:
Pluto, the ninth planet in our solar system,
was discovered by Clyde Tombaugh,
amateur astronomer, at Lowell Observatory,
Flagstaff, Arizona, United States of America,
on the eighteenth of February, 1930, at 3:58 p.m.
For many weeks, Mr. Tombaugh had taken photographs
of the same portion of the night sky, looking for the planet
Percival Lowell had surmised was at the outer edge
of the solar system, and which he had named "Planet X."
Comparing the photographs from successive nights,
he spied a 15th-magnitude image appearing and disappearing.
He knew that real stars show no shift in position,
but that a planet will show a slight shift of position, and thus
betray its planetary nature.
For three-quarters of an hour Mr. Tombaugh
was the only person in the world
who knew exactly the position of Planet X.
The new planet was named by eleven-year-old
Venetia Burney, of Oxford, England, who named it Pluto,

after the Roman God of the Underworld,
because Pluto receives very little light.

I had got all my information from reading *Boy's Own Annual.*
I sat down. The parents applauded.

Lahr said, "Thank you, James,
for that information. The study of science
is an important part of our curriculum
as we prepare these young people for the future world
they will live in." But he looked like he wanted to slay me.

At that moment I wished there was a trap door
in the floor of the classroom, just under Lahr's feet.
I would be holding the end of a string —
the other end attached to the trap door —
and as I pulled the string, *Vwap!* Lahr
would disappear through the floor.

On the way home,
　　　　Nora walked a bit ahead, dragging Addie.
Ran slapped me on the back. "Well done!
You had little Adolf slapping his boots in salute."

I guess that's a compliment.

Nora Loney

Papa came with us as far as the schoolhouse steps, but I knew
it was getting to be seven o'clock,
　　　　　　when Elmer would reopen the Buffalo.

Jim got his revenge, and educated Mr. Lahr on Pluto

at the same time. I grant him his courage;
I don't believe I could have done such a thing.

Susanna Payne played violin,
and I recited "The Song of Wandering Aengus"
by William Butler Yeats — a poem I love,
and Lahr let me,
            though it wasn't by his Mr. Blake.

By the time we left school, the wind
had changed to north,
                and snow was falling.
It was noticeably colder.
And Papa had missed Parent Night.

Gideon Freeman

Looked like they had a nice gathering
over at the schoolhouse. Mmn. Yes.

Mama always wanted me to go to school,
and I did, once we got to Oklahoma.
Got in a couple years' schooling there
before I became a young man and restless
to see what I could of the world.
Still, I can read the Bible,
and it's done me good. Yes.

But I don't go to no church. Hmpmh.
            Ain't no church in this town for my kind.
In there, they try to tame God,
make Him do tricks for 'em,
like a dog.

But a person can't tame God.
He's wild as a lion.
He'll haunt you.

They say, "May the Lord be with you."
It's as good as saying,
May the Lord *disturb* you.

Mmn. Yes.

George Loney now,
I'd say the Lord's with him.
I'd say the Lord's disturbing George Loney
real good.

Jim Loney

Effie won't let us go
to the Halloween dance party
at the Knights of Columbus Hall
behind the Catholic Church.

Even the Anglicans can go, if
their parents let them. Everybody else
who can't abide papists sends their kids
to the Presbyterian party.

Chester Grasswitch is going to hitch up his team
                    and take us on a hayride.
I'm going to be a newspaper boy.
I can wear regular clothes for that.
All I need is a newspaper.

Frank, being Catholic, finds us Presbyterians amusing.
Frank says we make up all our prayers out of our heads.
They keep theirs in a book.
He says Latin's better than English for talking to God.
Frank says he'll be a preacher for Halloween, says
all he needs is a Bible and a loud voice.

We were still talking about Halloween
when we took our seats in school.
First thing, Lahr called me to the front of the class.

"Mr. Loney. I believe you were to recite
a poem last night which you failed to do.
Tell me, do you have a mind like a sieve?"

I said nothing. My hands were still smarting
from Lahr's whapper.

"Let's see how much you can recall
of the poem you were assigned to recite.
Class, listen carefully as James recites his poem."

Lahr sat with his feet up on his desk,
holding his whapper across his left hand.
I turned to face the class.

Man was made for Joy & Woe;
And when this we rightly know
Thro' the World we safely go.
Joy & Woe are woven fine,
A Clothing for the Soul divine;
Under every grief & pine
Runs a joy with silken twine…

I sat down, waiting for what Lahr would do.

He cleared his throat, walked to the front of the room.
"Grade fours and fives to the chalkboard, this instant."

Addie Loney

Papa didn't come to Parent Night.
But Mama did.

II

The Funeral

Dr. John Payne

I've been the town doctor here in Argue
oh, about twenty years now.
I hear more secrets than the priest hears confessions.

For example, there's some rumbling about town
over Franz Lahr. He came here from Saskatoon
where a number of German Lutherans are settled.
His father is a Lutheran pastor up there.

Being German isn't contagious. It isn't a disease
they can contract. Nor is it a sin, particularly.
I'm no expert on sins; I just try
to heal the sick best I can.

Franz has a little secret of his own.
He was born with a cleft palate. Whoever sewed it up
after his birth did the job rather badly.
He tries to cover the scar by sporting a moustache,
but one side of his lip won't grow hair
so he shaves the other side to match. The result,
of course, is a moustache resembling the Führer's.

I'd stand up in church and defend Franz's right
to facial hair,
but I won't darken the door of any church.
Not since the polio outbreak of '37.

Imagine a disease that strikes mostly children.

I drove my Susanna up to Regina
all one oppressive August night.
Twelve years old.
I insisted on the best care money could buy.

She spent a year up there. I visited when I could.
I prayed every day.
Just like the Reverend Meany told me to do.

I wrote my prayers on little bits of paper
and folded them neatly in the pockets
of my frock.
Eventually, they filled up my pockets
like a gathering of moths.
I'd take them by the handful, let them fall
into the wastepaper basket
in a corner of my consulting room.
All the little prayers
floated down on their paper wings.

Susanna came home, a year older by the calendar,
older by a decade from her demeanor.

I remember how she swung those little legs,
her arms managing those crutches,
up the front steps of our house.

"What good were all my prayers?" I asked the Reverend.

Know what he said?
God helps those who help themselves.
That's what he said.

First I lost my Lily in childbirth.
Now my Susanna walks with crutches

and a brace on each leg.
If God waits around to see
if we can pull off miracles without him,
then I conclude
that God
is playing games with us.

Jim Loney

Papa works as dispatcher down at the depot.
Before Ran started working for the railroad,
none of us kids were ever allowed down there.

One day me and Frank and Tommy McGillivray wandered
over there, cupped our hands
and peered through the glass.
There was Pop at his big desk, not noticing us
at first, but soon as he did, Papa sprang out of his chair
faster than you can say Jack Robinson.
"You kids get the hell outa here!"
he roared, and off we dashed.

But one night, late — after we'd buried Mama —
I was out of bed, wandering the house.
Papa up, too. He took me by the hand
and we walked together into the April night,
down to the depot.
I sank into a corner chair.

I remember the calendar on the wall, the heavy glow
of the lamps,
the tall ticking clock — how it chimed ten times
and returned to ticking, regular as a heart.

Papa spoke into a telephone — we don't have one at home —
papers and notes tacked on the wall,
a typewriter in a corner.
Papa rolled in his chair from one thing to another.
In my sleepy head I heard the *tap-ta-tap-tap-ta-tap-tap-tap*
of the telegraph machine
and the squeal of the 10:15 train.
And then I was out like a light.

I woke in my bed, sun in my eyes,
wondering if I had dreamed it, this walk
down the dark streets with my father.
I thought he was so smart, so important,
working in his office.

I have never set foot in Papa's office since.

Addie Loney

Nora gave me the pail of scraps.
Said, FEED THE CHICKENS.
WATCH OUT FOR THAT WEASEL.
I made up a song.
        Weasel, weasel, stay away.
Turn around and around and around.
See if it's coming.

Chickens sing when they eat.
Feathers float up like snow
flying back to the sky.

Margaret Loney

There's my Addie — he thinks no one can see him,
tossing food scraps to the chickens,
standing on a wooden box at the end of the clothesline.
He's stopped now, turned his back on the hens.
He's reaching up into the clothes waving about him,
and inside his head, he is singing.

I know my Addie. He wants to wash
the meanness from her eyes —
that obdurate woman I refuse to name.
How my husband allowed the whole town to goad him
into letting a coarse woman like that
take over our household, I'll never know.

The sweet hands of Jesus were upon my Addie
the day he was born. It was the fever made him delicate.
How I sang to him night after night as he burned up
in his bed; how I prayed to Jesus to take my boy's fever,
and he did, but he took his own sweet time getting around to it.

That's when those hands started in, little fluttering
moth hands,
and now here he is, smelling the wash and hugging it all
with his moth hands, dusting everything
in soil.

Jim Loney

We had some snow after Parent Night,
and cold. Ran woke me Sunday morning, 4:15,
flung back the covers.

I shivered in the cold,
squinting in the lamplight at the clock.

"You're twelve, kiddo. You get to go hunting
with Pop and me."

Papa and Ran always said, until that instant,
I was too young to go hunting.

I put on two pairs of trousers and my wool shirt
over two undershirts, then my plaid coat.
Ran looked at me. "If you fall over, kid,
you won't be able to get up on your own."

We left everyone else sleeping. Especially Effie,
who'd have a hissy fit that we'd snuck out on the Lord's day.

Ran had packed a stack of mashed potato sandwiches,
an extra loaf of bread
and a pot of coffee.
I sipped some hot coffee on the porch and burned my tongue
waiting for Dr. Payne to drive up in his Buick.

I'd never ridden in a car like that. Velvet seats.
The light the headlights threw
bounced up and down the road. Dr. Payne
drove toward the low land, filled in
with wolf willow, cattails and cottonwood.

I sweated from the heat of the coffee.
My sweat turned to ice soon as we got out of the car
and crouched in the brush, waiting
for some sound of pheasants or guinea hens.

Night slowly lifted, like a fog,

and more things became visible. My hands, for instance,
one gloved and one not — must've fallen out of my pocket —
and colors, like the plaid in my coat.
And then birds began to rustle.

Papa showed me how to hold a shot gun
against my shoulder, aim and shoot.
When he was satisfied, he put a shell in.

We waited. And waited.
A pair of pheasants rustled, flew,
and Ran yelled, "Shoot 'em, Jim!"

I half stood and fired blindly into the air.
When I pulled myself out of the dirt
after the gun recoiled,
Dr. Payne exclaimed, "Did you see him go down?"
and slapped me on the back. We slogged
through the underbrush to take a look.

Papa said, "He's not big, but he'll be tender."
There he lay on the ground, his last breath
going out of him, the gay colors in his feathers,
the little ring at his neck.

It was the only bird any of us shot.
We drove back to town in silence, the pheasant
limp on the seat between me and Ran,
its feet curled into fists, the stench
of blood and buckshot in my nose.
My face hot.

I'm a man now, they said. Blinked over and over
to keep my watering eyes from spilling onto my face.

It had started, again, to snow. Hard, dry pellets
driving at the windshield.

Nora Loney

When we woke, Papa and the big boys
were nowhere to be seen. Effie was sufficiently enraged
so that by the time she came back to her senses,
we had missed Sunday School.
Addie and Effie and I dressed for church.
I stared out the window through a shower of snow.

Effie didn't abide anyone missing church. Papa refused always
but she bullied and badgered Ran to go.
We walked up the street to Knox Presbyterian,
Addie half skipping to keep up, Effie with a gathered-up face
ready to scare the devil out of anyone
who might ask where her men were.

Betty Shiflett was still putting up the hymn numbers.
Helen Davidson pumped the organ, and church started,
and the choir of vibrating voices marched down the aisle
as we sang *Holy, Holy, Holy.*

Reverend Meany had an exceptionally long sermon.
The edges of his teeth, tipped with gold,
shone in the light.
"Put on the armor of *righteousness*, the armor of *God.*"
He put his wide finger on the place in the Bible and poked at it.

Reverend Meany says we should be soldiers for God,
says his son, Milt, in gunnery training at Mossbank,
is a soldier for God.

“We know what God wants of us,” he declared,
solemnly closing the Bible.

Jim Loney

When Dr. Payne pulled up in front of our house,
Nora, Addie and Effie were walking home from church,
snow whitening the shoulders of their coats,
Effie building up like a blizzard
while Papa held up the pheasant like it was a trophy.

Effie scalded it. Nora had to pluck it.
All those fire-orange feathers.
It wasn't even as big as a regular chicken.

We ate it for dinner, quietly picking gunshot
from our teeth — the little startled sound
when they hit the plate,
no one daring to speak
for fear Effie would deal out God's wrath
for doing work on the Lord's day.

Gideon Freeman

I don't sleep so good in the night.
No. At first I wondered
if someone in the Loney family be ill.
The headlights lit the walls of my room
and then I saw the Loney boys leave
with the doctor. Yes.

Got myself up after that,
put some wood in the stove and warmed
my rooms.

Been here so long folks think I'm from here now. Mmhmm.

In the old days, they called us Buffalo Soldiers. Yes.
By the time I come north, buffalo was gone
but I was young, see, spent my days
down at Fort Assinniboine
blacksmithing and doing meanly chores
until we'd get orders to send someone home
over the Medicine Line.
See, the Indians,
they'd wander down from Canada, looking
for something that would feed 'em.
They'd stumble into Fort Ass
and we'd put a little meat in front of 'em
and then we'd take 'em back. Mhmm.

Wind moaned like something dying
through bones scattered over the land —
no trees, 'cept in the coulees.
And wind
ripped that boney brush right out the ground,
sent that sagebrush rolling and crashing
into the horses' legs,
manes and tails caught full o' burrs
till they went hard
like the faces on people been hungry a long time.

Oh, I remember like it was las' year. Mmhumh.

They trudged slowly back.
Enemy was wind and hunger.

Our horses, crossing the creeks,
would slip and break through the ice
and toss their heads wild-like.
And when the people forded the creeks,
they broke through
and jus' kept on walking. Yes.

I was dozy on my horse, Whiskey,
when we passed that pile o' rocks.
Dismounted. Led ol' Whiskey over to that pile
that marked the Medicine Line
and picked off a round, gray stone.

Put it in my pocket. For luck.

Susanna Payne

I was crutching home from school, my satchel
across one shoulder, when Ran Loney strode up.
His broad smile made me blush.
With a flourish,
he whipped out a lemon drop from his pocket.
I stopped and took his gift.
He lifted the satchel from my shoulder.

"I miss you at school." I hardly believed
I dared say it, and perhaps he didn't hear me.
The wind blew so fierce and raw.

Ran tucked his head and grinned at me.
"I don't miss Lahr."
We walked on toward my house,
my father still out on house calls. I said,

"What then will you do with yourself? Someone
as strong and smart as you
oughtn't stick around this place.
The world's your oyster."

We had come around my back door. The scent
of baked bread floated into the yard.

I bit my lip and asked him in,
knowing Mrs. Gabb would be in the house,
making it proper.
To my surprise, he accepted.

I swung my braced legs into the kitchen, saying,
"Ran's walked me home and carried my satchel.
Might we serve him tea?"
And Mrs. Gabb went all busy,
setting out a pot and two cups, then a plate
of her rolls, for which she is famous, of course.

Soon as she disappeared into the next room,
Ran leaned across the table.
"I want to tell you what I've decided.
You'll be the first to know."

I studied the fire in his eyes.
We've been friends, Ran and I, since before
my "illness," as my father calls it.
Ran defended me from others who would tease me
for my metal legs, though he drew some taunts himself
because of it. Were I a normal girl, I might
dare to think he cared for me.

"I rode with Howard Selemka up to Moose Jaw last week.
He's signed up.

Danny Filmore's signed up, too. Said he saw Howard
come home from the enlistment office
with a set of new clothes. Brand new boots.
Said he can't remember ever in his life
getting new boots.

So I've decided. I'm signing up.
There're flight schools opened up in Moose Jaw, and Regina."
He looked around the kitchen, through the window.
"I don't know when I'll go. But I've made up my mind.
When the right time comes, I'll be off."

I felt a mixture of happiness and dread. I rubbed my fingers
between the folds of my napkin.

"You want a new pair of boots, too?" I teased.
I was serious then. "You're only sixteen."

"To hear Howard tell it, they take one look at you
and send you to pick up your uniform. Howard says
they don't even look to see
if you've started to shave."

I stared out the window of our eating nook
at the trees stripped of their leaves from the wind,
and felt my eyes grow hot.

"I have a secret for *you*, Ran Loney." I hesitated.
"I… I'm teaching myself to walk. Without crutches."

His eyebrows lowered, puzzled.

"Every night when I go to bed I take off my leg braces
and set them in a corner of my bedroom.
Then I lean my crutches in the same place. I walk

toward my bed until I fall down.
Then I pull myself up and walk again.
In the morning, I make myself get out of bed
                and I walk toward my crutches and braces.
I'm going to do this until I don't fall down anymore.
I have a lot of bruises right now."

We both laughed.

                When he left, I stood
without my crutches, took three steps and turned
toward the door, my hand on the doorframe.
Ran turned on the step,
                        faced me, and kissed me.

Suddenly I could hardly feel any part of my body,
but for my hand on the doorframe,
and thought for one terrifying moment,
                        I might lose my grip.
I don't know if I smiled, or blushed,
or if I looked like some wild, uncouth thing standing there.
No words came from my mouth.

Oh, why! Randall Loney,
                        why did you do so rash a thing as that?
If I am never able to walk, what man will want me?
Now I will know always
                        the thrill of a kiss,
and know what it is I am cursed to live without.

Nora Loney

Effie appeared at the door of my bedroom.
"Where on God's green earth did you get a dress like that?
You got no business wearing such a thing."

It was Mama's dress. Mama's necklace.
I looked in the mirror and saw Mama, not myself.
As if Mama were standing right with me.
"It's for Halloween," I said.
I didn't know what kind of costume
                    it was supposed to be —
                                        Mama's best rose dress.
I hadn't yet put on the matching hat
with the bit of netting draped over the edge.

"You look like a shameless hussy. Take it off.
And where did you get a pearl necklace like that?"
She came close and inspected it with her fingers.
"Where in the wide world
                    did *you* get such a worldly possession?"

As though I'd stolen it. I felt as shamed as if I had.

"It was Mama's," I explained, as calmly as I could muster.
"It belongs to me now. Papa said."

"Very pretty." She began to smile and show her crooked tooth.
                    "Must have been expensive."

Then just as quickly, she frowned.

"What I could have if your father didn't drink up all my money.
Did anyone ever give *me* a pearl necklace? Nooo.
                                        Nobody's ever helped Effie out.

Well, here's one thing I want you kids to never forget —
you've got it so much better than I did.
At least you *have* a father."

Effie stomped noisily toward the kitchen.
I could hear her banging pots on the stove.

Jim stuck his head in the doorway of my room.
I grabbed Addie and we left the house
as quietly as we could.

Frank Selemka

Blizzard blew in.
So much for the hayride.

We hung around the Presbyterian hall
where Mrs. Meany had set up games.
I wanted to win at Cake Walk,
but to get a ticket you had to go up to Mrs. Meany
and recite a Bible verse.

I went back to Jim for help.
"Look, we'll split the cake, okay?" I said.
So Jim comes up with, "By His stripes we are healed,"
and I said, "By his stripes? That's a verse?
What's *that* supposed to mean?"
So then Jim says, "Okay. Try this one:
"Go ye and sin no more."
So I told it to Mrs. Meany.
It came out, "Go ye and sin more."

I could tell when Jim slapped his forehead I'd messed up.

He pulled me over. “Jesus wept,” he said,
both hands on my shoulders,
his eyes burning the verse directly into my brain.

I repeated it. Twice.
That’s when I said I’d bet the farm
the Catholics were having more fun.

Nora Loney

I knew there would be dancing
at the Catholic party. I confess
I wanted to see a real dance.

I found Addie and we left quickly
once Mrs. Meany’s back was turned.

Even through the howling snowstorm
we could hear the polka band playing
Roll Out the Barrel.
Inside, people were drinking beer. At church. Oh,
I just knew Effie would proclaim us sinners
and I already felt like one.

Danny Filmore strode up in his new uniform,
looking suddenly like a grown man,
and I wondered if it was Mama’s dress
or why he’d all of a sudden
noticed me, Ran’s kid sister.

I said I didn’t know the first thing about real dancing,
aside from our school dances, where we had a fiddler
and a caller who told us what to do.

He said it didn't take much to learn to polka.

Soon we were dancing to one song after another:
Pennsylvania Polka, Sweetheart Polka.
Addie filled himself up with deviled eggs
and fell asleep across the chairs
                    lining the edges of the room,
and I hadn't the foggiest notion what Jim was up to.

The war came home to me that night.
                                        Danny,
who had always been just another boy to me,
was leaving for training in a week.

Jim Loney

Me and Frank snatched up
a couple half-empty beer bottles
and went out in the snow,
            which had started to drift,
with more snow coming down by the minute.

We tried the beer — dark and yeasty and vile,
but were happy about the snow,
and built ourselves a snow fort in front of St. Jude's,
and raised the walls thicker and higher the more
                              the snow came down.

Frank started to shake his bottle, his thumb over the mouth,
and let the froth fly and freeze
over the sides of the fort. The effect
was so keen, I shook my bottle.
            By then, Tommy McGillivray'd come out.

Tommy ran back and forth, swiping bottles
from tables and under chairs
until we had the entire fort covered
                                        in frozen beer froth.
It was beautiful.

Glad to find my other glove in my pocket.
Wondered how it got there.
A few older boys from school
                                came up to inspect our work,
eggs in their pockets already frozen, useless
for throwing at anything, said,
                                "What a waste of good beer."

As they walked away, Tommy said,
"My boogers are frozen inside my nose,"
and we realized how cold we were,
that the snow had nearly stopped,
and how the frigid night air
had sunk down from the north
                                like the White Zombie
and invaded our town.

Frank Selemka

My dad found us
behind the walls of our fort,
saw the beer bottles lined up in rows like a platoon,
yanked me up by my sleeve,
            slapped me upside the head,
my tuque flying off into the snow.

The beer on his breath and mine

made me dizzy. I stumbled home
with him behind me,
afraid of his butcher's hands
          with their dark fur
inside his gloves,
his eyebrows white with frost,
his voice booming like a Halifax
on a bombing run.

Jim Loney

The polka band grew loud and soft again
as the door opened and closed, and Nora
came outside, Danny carrying Addie, asleep,
and Nora calling our fort a *castle*,
for crying out loud.

Damn. Effie wasn't asleep when we got home.
She stood at the door with her mouth open, beer smell
rising into her hairy nostrils, her eyebrows
jacked up high on her forehead
          like somebody'd yanked her hair straight up.

                              I tried shoving my clothes
and my beer-frozen gloves into the wardrobe,
but decided they'd make everything else in there
                                        stink like beer.

I cleared out my dresser drawer of clean clothes
and stuffed them in there. Closed the drawer.
Then I ran my hands and feet under warm water
till they ached like the dickens,

but for the life of me, I couldn't get that beer smell
off my hands.

Nora Loney

That night, my blood came.
Seeing it there between my legs, staining
the cloth like a wound, I cried, not knowing
if I should feel happy to be a woman,
or terrified, knowing that the dishes, stove, floors,
the boiling and ironing of clothes
would be my life sentence.

Ice and snow clotted my bedroom window.
The wind swept the dark clouds
through our town and out again.
Papa off doing what Papa does.

Night pressed on me with its frigid fingers,
the bedsprings prodding the underside of me.
I cried myself to sleep, covered with a blanket
of emotions, for Danny, for me, my arms
crossed over my breasts.
Slept hard and heard nothing.

I should have heard Papa cry, *Woman!*
And her say, *You're doing this to spite me,*
aren't you? You're doing this to see how far
you can drive me into the ground, George Loney.
And before she closed the door
and the lock clicked
like a cold and final curse,
Get thee behind me, Satan.

I should have felt the outside air
steal into the house, and wakened.
            I should have wakened.

Morning, it was Addie found Papa
            curled on the step like a ham.

Little Addie with his odd ways going to open the door
for reasons only Addie knows.

I should have heard the crack
of her frozen heart, the door's eternal judgment
or his slow paling, whiskey rising
                        from his pores
as he grew gray and silent as tin.

Jim Loney

I heard him swagger home. I lay in bed
with my hands tucked in my armpits, watching my breath
                                    steam the room.
I heard his off-key singing
                    muffled all of a sudden,
as if he'd fallen in the snow, and I thought,
bet he's gone and fallen into our fort and wrecked it.
                    But I guess he'd got himself up
because I heard him, clear,
            Bringing in the Sheaves, top of his lungs.
Everybody in town must have heard it.
Then the variations,
                    the ones us kids made up
and Effie made us memorize a whole chapter
of Romans for: *Bringing in the Sheets*,

and *Eating Gouda Cheese, We shall come rejoicing…*

Heard an argument as usual. Door open and close,
and I thought, *He's inside.*

Who would leave a person, who would do that —
like a wash tub you lean beside the house and never
think about till you want it.

And where was Freeman?

Gideon Freeman

Yes. I'm usually out at night.
But I gone in by that time. Made a fire.
See, it was cold.
The kind o' cold that turns your head to ice,
freezes your pant legs stiff. Yes.

And I'm getting old, and that old
don't take to winter. Not the kind we have.
I seen Mrs. Lim take out the garbage
behind the New Moon.
She say to me, "Don't slip on this snow, Mr. Freeman,
and I say, "I sure don't want to do that,"
and I say good night.

I seen them boys in front of St. Jude's
having a grand ol' time. Heard the polka band.

If I'd seen George Loney out,
I'd have helped him home as usual. Yes.

I'd have heard him coming home, 'cept
I had my good ear down on the pillow — bad ear up,
the one where I lost the eardrum
down at Fort Ass.

Mr. Loney, I always felt for him.
He got a lot of past in him, Mr. Loney does.
And when a person got too much past in him,
he does what Loney does.

Elmer Spanner, Proprietor, Buffalo Bar

I see George Loney every night but the Lord's.
Comes in, stands here at the bar, orders a rye. Hell,
that's about all I got. Rye.
Pretty damn near same guys in here all the time.
Government says I got to close five to seven.
Don't want trouble,
so I do.
Before five, George stands here at the bar, drinks his rye.
After seven, he sits over there, drinks his rye.
I've known George
ever since he had that farm. Nice little farm.
He'd stop in whenever he come to town.
Losing that farm was George's greatest failure
but wasn't his fault. Gawdam drought.
Gawdam dust. Gawdam government.

So after eight, ten drinks, George
curls up under the table, takes a nap
in the sawdust.
Looks pretty cozy under there.
When the CPR comes in, I wake him up,

say, “Hey! George! Train’s come in.
Time to go to work.” And George
shuffles off to the depot
with sawdust dropping off him.

Well, Halloween night, storm come through. Damn cold.
Catholics having a big party,
          we just had heathens in here.
Fight broke out. Poker game.
Seemed like George was sleeping like a dog
                              when it broke out.
George didn’t get his whole nap. Fight woke him up
before he’d slept it off. Had another shot
and left.

That’s the last I saw of him.

Father Andrew Innes

I saw George Loney that night
                              fall into the snow.
I was up late, with what they call “writer’s block” —
trying to write something that could remotely be called
a sermon. Our churches — Anglican and Roman —
sit across from each other on opposite corners.

Clara and I, we live in the Anglican manse
                                        next door to the church.
          And yes,
                    I saw him, from my window, fall
into the boys’ snow fort in front of St. Jude’s.

When I see George Loney, I see Christ carrying His cross.

We are all stumbling and falling under our own crosses,
those carved from our hands, our sweat,
and those not of our own making.

I felt moved to throw on my coat
and pull George out of the snow.

At first he didn't really see me. He was saying to himself,
Maggie, I'm sorry, you know I'm sorry,
and he turned to see who was lifting him up.
Oh, it's you … Father … bless me Father for I have sinned.
He chuckled.

I chuckled with him, brushed some of the snow
and sawdust off of him,
set him on his feet and on his way.

All it would have taken was to walk with him.
As Christ asks us to walk with Him.

All it would have taken.
Was just to walk him home.

Addie Loney

Woke up.
It was quiet.
I stood by Nora's bed.
Watched Nora
till she woke up.

She made me warm milk and porridge.

I ran to the door
'cause I saw in the window
a bunch of magpies in a tree.

If I run out the door
and wave my arms,
the magpies fly.

Looks like the whole tree
rising into the sky.

Nora Loney

Ran was working the train to Moose Jaw
so Jim dressed and walked past his ruined fort
and collected John Argue
from the Mercantile.

Don Payak was in the store.
He put on his hat with the ear mufflers
and his shoveling gloves. They came and raised Papa
off our front step, his knees
hard frozen to his chest.

They laid him down in the Mercantile
in front of the stove, on Mr. Payak's old war cot.

The store smelled of creosote and coffee,
and little aprons of white circled the floor
beneath the sacks of flour.

Jim Loney

Took three days till we could straighten his legs,
his arms, his head. The frost
on his eyebrows melted and dripped into his eyes,
then spilled like tears.
His ears turned from white to gray.

We stayed around Papa as much as we could.
When Effie walked in, she shooed us back to school,
but we'd sneak out again and go see
what Papa was doing
lying in front of the stove. Some days
I'd stay most of the day, listening to the men talk
about Papa and how far back they went.

But I was in the store when Dr. Payne showed up,
looked down on Papa and pronounced him dead,
signed the certificate, then drove away in his Buick
toward the Childress farm,
leaving white tracks
that came together far down the section line road.

Nora Loney

On the fourth day Helen Davidson,
with the graceful hands of an organist,
laced Papa's fingers together over his chest.

The town wandered in and out like a wake;
every boy from school, and a few of the girls,
had to come and catch a glimpse of him.

None of us dared remove his overcoat.

Reverend Meany said Papa had no right
to be buried inside the cemetery fence
because he refused church, because he was a drunk.

Otto Selemka held his hands together over the stove
and over Papa like some kind of baptism
and reminded everyone Papa was a veteran
    of the Great War.

Then Lester Spotts walked down to the cemetery,
piled straw and twigs on the spot
        beside Mama's grave
and set it on fire and that was it.
Papa and Mama would lie side by side.

Effie cried noisily whenever anyone was near
but never said she'd shut the door,
believing no one knew.

I feared that Jim
    would blurt out the truth.

What would she do to us then?

Ran Loney

I pulled out Pop's only suit,
faded in patches and frayed at the cuffs.
The one he wore at Mama's funeral.

We set him in the coffin Lester built

from scrap lumber he had back of his barn,
and we carried him down the road, past
the scuffed and tired houses on the street,
carried him up the steps he died on,
and lifted him onto the kitchen table,
                    where I washed him,
but couldn't wash away the black seams
         in the cracks of his hands
or the frostbite white of him.

Then I shaved him, dressed him in the suit
and combed back his hair.
Anybody could take one look at him and see
he had been broken in his life.

In the front room of the house
         I heard Father Innes talking,
sitting with Effie who was blotting out her chair,
a King James Bible on her downward-sloping lap.

I heard the train squeal to a stop down at the station,
hissing as though letting out a held breath,
and all was quiet again. There is something like grief
in such stillness and silence.
                              The trains
would stop and start and go on their way now
across the endless prairie
without Pop.

Nora Loney

In the end, Father Innes buried Papa,
since Reverend Meany refused,

though Father Dominic also offered to do it,
but Effie was dead set against "an RC funeral."

Father Innes opened a book
as we stood over the grave, the black earth
gaping like a mouth as he read, *The Lord's mercy*
is on those that fear Him
from generation to generation,
and the word *fear* rang in me like a stone.

Then we sang:
O joy that seekest me through pain,
I cannot close my heart to thee;
I trace the rainbow through the rain,
And feel the promise is not vain,
That morn shall tearless be.

And our trembling voices blew away on the wind.

That night when all the stars looked down
on everything we had done,
I felt the cold settle over my bed and wakened,
the whole of the house frigidly cold.

I crept about
to discover Addie nearly frozen himself,
knotted up asleep
in front of the open door.

I carried him to bed with me, folded myself
around him, stroked his head beneath my chin,
and knew what he had done.

He had let Papa in.

Ran Loney

I remember the day Pop came home
  with a second-hand bike,
and after supper, in summer's long light,
held the seat while I wobbled down the lane,
his farmer's hand balancing my seven-year-old frame.
I want to think he coaxed, patient, until
I gave up believing in gravity
and believed in him,
the faith of thrust and flight.

But the liquor on him sickened the air.
He pitched forward, running to keep up,
his balance as shaky as mine,
until I planted myself in the hard-packed ground.
He swore and stomped off toward the house
where he and Mama swerved
    and teetered on their marriage,
the future already rising up against them.

Outside in the dying light
I tottered, crashed, and pushed off again
until the air held me in its fist.

For the first time, but not the last.

Nora Loney

There's a photograph of me with Mama and Papa —
taken when I received a Bible one Sunday
as I was confirmed in the church.

Papa is smiling, as though his sadness
had become a bird and flown away
to sit and sing on a fencepost.
Mama and I resemble each other, and I
do not yet hold in my face
traces of regret, the way
Mama's and Papa's faces
are lined with small and deep regrets.

This photograph is the one sign I hold to myself,
to believe they valued me, a girl, enough to stand
for this moment with me
apart from my brothers.
In this frame contains my anchor —
that I was treasured,
not for the shirts I would learn to sew
or the eggs I could fry,
but for me. Myself.

Because of this, I hold out the possibility of God.

Margaret Loney

It was hail that broke my George's heart.
Not drought, or grasshoppers. Hail.

With drought it was like this: you planted,
and wheat came up, and it'd come to June —
hotter and hotter,
and still no rain. A week, two weeks, then three.
Then wind, oven-hot. All that wheat
just baked there on the stalk. No crop.
But you could see it coming.

You were ready.

With grasshoppers it was like this:
they always moved in from the south.
A few at first, then hundreds, thousands,
like locusts in the Bible.
You'd set foot outside and they'd spring up
all around you. But you knew
they were coming, so your mind was ready.

But the hail. Oh, my glory. The hail.
This was in '34. Three small children
and Addie on the way.
And it was a beautiful crop.
How it swayed in the fields, how it rippled
like waves on an ocean, far as we could see.
We'd start with the binder in two days.

That afternoon I heard George running in the door —
and that word forming on his mouth before I heard it: *hail.*

He pointed west, where a great purple cloud was blooming
like a rose.
Oh, it was big. *Hail* was all George could say. *Hail.*

I called for the children. I called, *Get the chickens in.*
Ran and Nora and Jim rushed in,
the chickens ahead of them,
all rushing in the door like a wind.

I'll never forget how suddenly it turned so cold.
It came straight for us. It roared.
All of us huddled in the house, so dark
we couldn't see each other's faces,
and the chickens cowering by the stove

as it came down and down.

Then, it stopped.
I found myself pressing Jim into my apron.
A rush of rain.
And the storm rolled away like a wagon
crossing a bridge.
The sun came out. We shooed the chickens
out the door and looked around.

All our wonderful wheat, the whole quarter section
flattened and muddied.
Buried under hail and mud.
Not a bushel left over. Not even a handful
to put in a vase like a bunch of daisies.

That's when everything went to smash.
That's when George felt like God was playing with him
just for spite.
He sat in his chair by the front window
and stared. I couldn't even coax my George into eating.

Finally he got up and went out to the barn.
I could hear him in there,
hitching Nellie up to the buggy.
I watched George and the buggy and pretty Nellie
get smaller and smaller
as they drove up the section line road toward town.

George didn't come back till after dark.
Unhitched Nell, came in and sat at the table.
He was drunk,
but I couldn't blame him then.

It was like this: after a bit, I wiped my hands on my apron

and sat down there at the table.
He said he'd been to the lawyer, told him
to find a buyer for the farm before
                    the bank claimed it. Told him,
find someone to buy the team of horses.
Then my George put his head into his hands
and sobbed. Softly, like a child.

As I'm here as God's witness, I say
it wasn't the war that broke George Loney.
It was hail.

Ethel Meany

Of course, we brought food to the house.
Casseroles, upside-down cakes.
We entered, passed the little table holding the open Bible,
laid our gloves beside it. We carried our baking
into the kitchen, and I gasped.

"Oh, my dear," I said. "I never knew
                    you didn't have an *electric* range!"
Still stoking an old cast-iron stove!

We sat with Effie on the needlepoint chairs, made tea for her
while the big clock struck each painful minute.

Effie said, "I'll be all right. The Lord knows
                    what I've been through.
The Lord gives me all the strength I require."

Poor Effie patted her eyes.
"I know the Lord helps those who help themselves."

I patted her knee. "Everything works out for the best,"
I assured her. And of course, we all agreed.

Margaret Loney

I've wandered the streets of town, restless,
skimmed the sloping floor of the Mercantile,
wrung my hands.
I've hovered over the funeral, the open grave.
I've heard it all.

What really would have made my blood boil,
had I had any left to boil,
was those church circle ladies —
they've always put on airs, thought they were better,
not ever having lived on a farm.
Well, believe you me, they know not a thing
about a Majestic stove.

See, we got maybe $1,500 for the farm.
$100 for the team of horses.
It was just enough to buy this house outright,
but George said, "Maggie,
they got the power in town.
You can have one of those plug-in ranges."

I didn't know the first thing about an electric stove,
but I knew my Majestic. My bread came out
so high, just golden-brown,
and smelling like heaven.

The last thing our team of horses did
before Al Hardy bought them

was to haul my Majestic the twelve miles to town.
Any truck would've broken down with that load.
But George and Ran gave a *Heeyup! Ike! Heeyup! Nell!*
And off they went.

I didn't much like being stuck in town,
expected to join women's groups,
with all their pettiness.

At least I didn't have to try to get used to a new stove.

III

The Train

Franz Lahr

Amazing how the soup pots of small towns
are just waiting to boil over anything at all.

After all the stories in the papers
about citizens boycotting Italian stores and restaurants
in cities like Toronto and Winnipeg, along comes
                    Air Marshall Italo Balbo,
come to the rescue of British troops.

The editorial applauded Balbo's humanity,
but emphasized that one's Italian and German neighbors
still must be watched
                    and reported to authorities if necessary.

That's when I walked into the classroom
with a newspaper in my hand.

We had a little discussion about *propaganda.*
I wrote it in large letters on the chalkboard.
Asked for a definition. Received none.

Forty-four children, several even talking of joining up,
and they wouldn't know *propaganda* if it were a rabid dog
bit them in the face.

I suggested a definition: "Deceptive or distorted information
that is systematically spread." Why?
The need to have a populace that is *afraid.*

Contrary to popular belief,
your neighbor isn't your enemy
just because he eats spaghetti.

Of course, all the children went home and promptly
told their parents what I'd said at school.

Next day the RCMP showed up. Again.
I told them, "You've already searched my shack.
Would you like to check my sock drawer for grenades?"

That was it. Now I'm required to report
to a probation board in Regina once a month.

Mary-Ann Meany is not allowed to speak with me.

Ethel Meany

I walked into the post office
and there was Carol talking with Agnes Lockhart.
I announced right then and there
that we were no longer allowing our Mary-Ann
to see that Franz Lahr.

The whole world knows
Agnes is the biggest gossip in town, and now
everyone will know the Meanys
won't abide a German spy here in Argue.
Our Mary-Ann was unhappy about it,
but we — my husband and I —
have our reputation to uphold.

Agnes says she's making sure everyone knows

the man who has undertaken to teach our children
is under surveillance by the authorities.

"Doesn't that make your blood run cold?" she said.

Jim Loney

Living with Effie is like trying to sneak your hand
under the hen to get the egg before she starts
pecking you to death.
It's a trick, that's for sure.

Effie won't let us play Mama's gramophone.
She says, "You take that heathen music off this minute.
Only music that belongs in a Christian home is God's music."

Mama loved *Madame Butterfly*.
I doubt Mama had ever been to see an opera in her life,
but she loved the whole idea of opera.

Once I asked her what opera was, and she said it was
as if, instead of saying everything, you sang it.

That day, we sang everything, Mama and me.
Ran shook his head and rolled his eyes, but eventually
he started in, and Nora, too.

We sang about the bread in the oven.
We sang about setting the table.
We sang about how good supper tasted.

Mama said, in an opera, you have to sing while dying.
I threw myself on the floor and pretended to die, singing.

Even Papa laughed that night.

I miss the gramophone.

Addie Loney

Now the gramophone's curled up
like a big sleeping bird.

Nora Loney

I was sprinkling shirts for ironing
when we heard a knock at the door.

It was a stranger.
"Madam," he said when Effie answered,
I see that you are a God-fearing family.
I see that right away because of the open Bible
you have in your entranceway.
I know that I am talking to Christian people here,
and I can see in your face
that you bear the love of God
and that you have accepted Jesus Christ
as your Lord and Savior."

Effie said, "If you're selling something,
I'm not interested. I'm a poor widow
with four children to raise, and my dinner is burning."

Then the man again. "Madam, I have been sent here
as a missionary for God.

It was the very hand of the Lord
that led me to your door, knowing by faith
that you are a God-fearing woman."

Effie had to invite him in or tell him to go away,
or the whole frozen creation
would wander inside and sit at the table, as she says,
and so they sat in the front parlor
            with the gramophone between them.

That was the start.

"Madam, I am certain you will be interested
in one or more of these new Bibles
I am spreading unto all the land.
Now, I know you may say, 'But sir,
                        I already have a Bible,'
but I ask you to look deep into your heart.
How can you have too much of the Word o' God?"

She invited him to stay for supper.

His name was Elijah. Elijah Small.
            He wasn't at all small — thin and tall,
with what Mama would call a Baptist face,
                        and little crooked teeth.

Effie spooned him extra potatoes and smiled.

Mouth full of food, Elijah asked us,
                "What did Jesus say to the crippled man?"

Jim and I looked at each other. Jim shrugged.

"Jesus said, 'Take up thy bed and walk.'"

"What? That makes no sense," Jim says.

Effie's eyes narrowed. Lines formed
            like a plowed field around her mouth.

"Jim knows a number of Bible verses, don't you, Jim?"
I said, kicking him under the table.

"Um, yeah, if thy foot causes thee to stumble,
cut it off, for it is better to enter the Kingdom of Heaven
with one foot than to suffer in Hell,
                        and if thine eye causes thee to stumble,
            pluck it out, for it is better — "

"Enough!" cried Effie.

"I can see you have taught your children
            to love and fear the Lord," grinned Elijah Small.

Jim Loney

The Bible salesman stayed three days.
He took a room at the King George Hotel
                        but ate at our house,
and sat in our parlor with Effie.

Mornings, we went to school.
            Afternoons, he was in our parlor,
like God had plucked him up by the back of his collar
and dropped him there
with the suitcase of Bibles between his feet.

Ran came home from his Regina run, said,

"Who the hell is this guy?"

"I come from good Christian stock, like you,"
Elijah Small said, helping himself to extra turnips.
"Yessirree, my father was a preacher.
Baptist.
But we suffered something terrible these last years,
because no one had money to pay my daddy.
But even with all that, no food on the table and all that,
I dedicated my life to becoming a missionary for the Lord."

"My father left us when I was two," Effie said.
"Mother said he was dead, but I found out later."

Didn't seem Elijah was listening.
"I'm spending the rest of this winter down in California,
bringing the Word o' God
to those who have ears to hear."

I imagined long ears of corn sticking out of his ears.
I thought he looked pretty good that way.

Addie Loney

When we got home from school,
Effie was putting clothes in a suitcase.
That preacher man came.

Mama said, "Now, Addie, dear,
quietly now — go get my pearl necklace
out of that suitcase.
That's it, reach down —
under the blue dress.

That's my boy."

Put it in my cigar box.
Mama liked that.

Margaret Loney

I peeked into the briefcase of Bibles.
Same two Bibles he waves in the air,
and a bottle of moonshine.

Effie rushed about
                    taut and apprehensive as a hen,
that shyster Bible salesman
standing in the middle of the floor, waiting.

I knew what she was looking for:
                    George's drinking money.
I hid it. She won't find it in this house.

Nora and Jim stood in the kitchen
looking at each other, at Effie
clucking every time she picked up
                    the edge of a mattress,
shook out George's shoes,
turned his coat pockets inside out.

"It's here somewhere —
I just bought this new hat with it."
I took great satisfaction in the agitation in her voice,
but wished she'd not used it on my children
when she turned on them, said,
                    "I've told Mr. Small the truth

about you little heathen — that you're not mine,
that I was only here to try to save you little brats
from frying in H-E-L-L.
Well, go fry. I'm leaving."

Elijah Small took out his pocket watch,
tapped its face, cleared his throat.

George floated near the ceiling, useless.
Nearly a month dead and he can't even
get himself to the floor.

It was I threw open the door
just as the Thursday afternoon train
opened its steel mouth and sang.
And it was I closed the door after them.

Halleluiah. Play the gramophone.

Ran Loney

It was a bright, frozen day. One of those days
that makes you squint as though it's summer,
though day starts shutting down
a little after three.

From the windows of the New Moon
I saw Effie and that stranger — tall, in a dark felt hat
too large for his head,
suitcases in both his hands.

By the time I ran up our front steps and tossed
my coat and hat onto the coat tree,

the blinding, bright day
had curled up to sleep like a cat.

Nora and Jim stood in the kitchen
like people milling around a train station
waiting for someone to make an announcement.

I said, "So, is she gone for good?"

Carol Williams

"So, that's the way the cookie crumbles," Agnes said to me.
She'd just seen with her own beady eyes
Effie Slade get on the train
with that Bible salesman from Alberta.

"Well," I said, sorting letters into boxes,
"is she going for a little bit or forever?"

"How should I know?" Agnes answered.
Her eyebrows crunched together,
and the wrinkles on her face stood out like a net.

She stuck her face through the bars of my postal station.
"Me, I wouldn't try for a minute
to be a mother to children not my own.
Now, I remember how Margaret
used to ride herd on that crew, and nothing —
mind you, not a thing — got past her.
But since then, they've just run wild.
I wouldn't be a bit surprised
if it was those children ran her off."

Nora Loney

We looked at each other and wondered what to do.
Then Jim let out a whoop.

Ran said, "We eat supper, that's what we do."

We had most of a loaf of bread,
two potatoes. More sprouting down in the cellar.
A few eggs. The chickens
had mostly stopped laying because of the cold.

I sliced the bread, cracked the eggs, dipped
the bread in the eggs and fried it.
We ate the bread with syrup.
It wasn't enough for Ran and Jim.

After supper, we searched around the house
looking for Papa's drinking money. Found none.

Ran said, "We'll do fine. I'm working."

Then we cranked up the gramophone.
Addie fell asleep in my lap. We stayed up late.

In the morning, cold had settled firmly in the house.
No one had got out of bed in the night
to fire the furnace or stoke the stove.
Effie'd done that.

We ate cold cereal and walked to school.

Jim Loney

After Lahr dismissed us,
we went home to our stone-cold house.
I went down to the basement and stoked the furnace.
First paper, then kindling, a shovel of coal,
and finally lit it all,
blew on it to give it life.

I moved upstairs and lit a fire in the stove, then
outside to play
while Nora and Addie shopped at the Mercantile
for porridge, cocoa, a tin of meat — what
Ran's eighty-five cents would buy.
He emptied the money from his pockets
before heading off to his three-day shift.

In the morning the house was frigid cold.
I never thought to wake or go down
and feed that monster furnace. Nora
woke early, built a fire in the stove
and made porridge, which she burned,
and it tasted just like burn.

Everyone in town knows what happened to us.
Don't need fire to spread a rumor.
Some already saying we'll be going
to live with relatives. What relatives?
Only one I know about is Mama's sister, Louise.
Lives in Ontario — big brick house — and five children.

I doubt she'll want the likes of us.

Ran Loney

I rode up to Moose Jaw on my shift,
watched guys in their new khakis and boots
not even scuffed yet, waving their hats
out the windows at parents and girlfriends,
big goofy grins on their faces,

and decided I would ride this stretch of black-ridged fields,
pass these plodding little towns
with their school and their churches, each spire
trying to outdo the other,

each bar named Buffalo or Antelope or Stockman —
I would pass these only once more, and then in uniform.

I had seven hours in the city before my train
was to squeal and clank through the rail yard,
pick up steam and turn back south. Gave me time enough
to visit the enlistment office.

I filled out the forms. No one asked my age.
Everyone knows it's the best job going,
will keep a guy in beer and cigarettes
with plenty left over to send home.

Now with the Americans declaring war,
excitement's at fever pitch.
Now's my time to make a break.

I don't want to die in Argue, Saskatchewan.
If I die, may it be in some distant place,
testing the limits of my endurance.

But when I took our front steps two at a time

and burst in the front door
with a duffel bag filled with my uniform and boots,
the look on Nora's face
was as if I'd died.

Father Andrew Innes

Our son Adam came home from school with news
that since the bombing of Pearl Harbor,
those Japanese living on the coast
are now required to turn over their automobiles
and close their stores.
Apparently, Franz has been reading newspapers
to the children.
It was our son's passion for automobiles
that caught his attention.

Louise Gillingham came to my office beside the church
to express her opinions of the schoolteacher.
"After what the Japs did to Pearl Harbor," she said,
they should all be rounded up and deported
back where they came from,
and that young teacher
acts as though the Japs are anything *but*
our enemies."

Well, Clara came in the door mere minutes later
to say Louise and other citizens of our town
have been meeting secretly
to decide how to dispense with the schoolteacher.

I stood up in the pulpit Sunday morning
and read from Ezekiel 37.

God tells Ezekiel to take two sticks: write "Israel"
on one, "Judah" on the other. God
directs Ezekiel to join the two sticks together
"that they may become one in your hand."

I said, "While God tries to bring us together,
we have done our best
to pull ourselves apart.
As the Apostle Paul tells us,
we are no longer Jew or Gentile, slave or free,
and, I may add, Canadian
                    or Japanese or German.
We may be at war, the likes of which
we have never known in this age,
                    but *we are God's people*,
that we may be one in God's hand …"

At this, I made a fist and held it in the air.

Franz Lahr

They waited until nearly eleven o'clock —
after the rest of Argue had gone to bed.
There came a knock on my door that just about
rattled the whole rickety house apart.

Seven or eight men stood outside
in heavy black coats, hats pulled low over their eyes.
I could make out only shadows.
No moon, only a fine spray of stars in the sky.

Said they'd had a little meeting.
Said they didn't want no gawdam

German teacher in this town,
and if I didn't get myself out of Argue by morning,
they'd be more than happy
to *escort* me out of town.

I stood shivering in my nightclothes,
my hands fingering the faulty latch
given to locking on its own,
the key lost long ago.

I don't know how I had the presence of mind
to remind those gentlemen
that the next train wouldn't arrive for another day,
and if they could see to it to grant me one day,
I would be off.

I am certain
Mary-Ann Meany's father was among them.

Reverend Albert Meany

I stood in the pulpit this morning
and preached the word of God to my congregation.

"Brethren in Christ," I began, "you know
that I have been placed here among you
to witness to the inerrant truth of the Bible.
I believe someone among us
was sent to our town for a purpose,
and it is this: he was placed here by God as a test.

Yes, a test. Be ye certain of this — that God
puts His children to the test,

to see if we are indeed soldiers for God,
or if we have fallen, like the people of Ninevah, into sin
and complacency.

Do not doubt that God tests us to see if we are faithful
unto Him.
Our country has gone to war
to drive the Devil from our midst.
To defeat him.
He will appear in disguise, my friends,
and don't be fooled!
The Devil is oh, so clever.

God calls us to cast out the Devil amongst us
that we may be cleansed,
that we may be made righteous,
that we may be made acceptable
unto God.

This we have done.
Praise the Lord!
Praise God in His holy sanctuary!"

Jim Loney

Ran sat dressed in uniform,
his cap over one knee,
drumming the arm of the chair with his fingers.
The knee with the cap on it jigged up and down
like a little man on a bumpy train.

Addie leaned into Ran
as if Addie could soak him up before he left.

The clock loomed over us. Its steady ticking.
We all kept looking at it. Didn't need to —
the train's whistle would tell us
when it was time.

I knew if Nora started to cry,
we'd all be done for.
She sliced bread in the kitchen, buttered the slices,
set thick slabs of meatloaf onto the bread.

Meatloaf she made for supper last night.
With mashed potatoes.
An extravagance, Nora called it.

Wrapped the sandwiches in waxed paper,
folded the ends into a triangle,
tucked them under.
Nora did it all so slowly,
it seemed like we were in some kind of time warp,
like in *The Zombie's Curse*
Frank and I read together.

I thought to play the gramophone, but then decided
if we wanted to keep our tears in our heads,
playing the gramophone was not a good idea.

I bit my fingernails to the quick
until the train's whistle cut through us.

Ran stood up. Picked up his duffel.
Set his cap on his head.

Without a word.

Nora Loney

We walked Ran to the train.
I held his free hand. Addie held mine.
Jim grasped the duffel slung over Ran's shoulder.

We continued in this manner, looking ahead, not at each other,
over the lumpy, frozen ground,
the wind numbing our faces.

Freeman was on the platform
                        walking the length of the train,
                                    a lantern in one hand.
Freeman, swinging it, saw Ran in his uniform,
                        the rest of us hanging onto him,
and that lantern stopped,
                                    suddenly, in its arc.

He shook Ran's hand, flashed his big, kind smile.
It was too much for me. My tears came.

I tried to say, *Write. Please. Please.*
I could say nothing.
The only sounds coming from my mouth
were what no civilized person would recognize as speech.

And then he was in his seat at the window.
The fingers of his hand touched the glass tenderly.
                                                            I felt it
as if he had touched my face.

Then he was gone.

Ran Loney

My neck ached from twisting my head
halfway behind me
to watch my brothers and sister,
the shabby houses of Argue
grow smaller,
the prairie grasses
up to their necks in snow,
fallow fields drifted white
from horizon to horizon.

I'd left town on this train dozens of times.
But not like this.
When I could no longer keep my tears at bay,
I faced the window and hid my shame.

Wally Stevens came through to punch tickets,
sat down in the seat beside me.
"Son," he said,
"I've seen 'em all. Seen 'em worse than you.
You've seen 'em, too.

Go ahead, kid. Let 'em come."

I cried like a boy who'd smashed his new bike.
Wally patted my shoulder.
Then he got up, punched the tickets
of the other passengers in the car.

Ten minutes later he was back,
pulled a cold bottle of root beer
from inside his jacket.

"Sorry it ain't the real thing, kid," he said,
"but you'll get that soon enough."

Addie Loney

Ran got swallowed
by the train.

Mr. Lahr, too.

IV

Christmas

Mary-Ann Meany

Father and Mother and I
had another argument over the Sunday roast beef
about my wanting to apply to Regina College.
I finished my grade twelve a year ago.

Mother said, "College is not a good place
to find a husband right now, dear.
All the good young men are fighting a war."

Father said, "I'm saving up for your brother
to go to college.
You know what happens to young ladies in a big city.
You know what they become. We've discussed this.
I don't want it mentioned again."
His eyes pierced me.

I wanted to say, *Yes, Father, what do they become?*
Whores? Is that the word you won't say?
What am I now?
What is it that you make me
when you slip into my bedroom late at night?

I don't know if I will ever be able to say those words.
I am terrified of my father.

After the cherry pie, which I had made,
I went for a walk, wrapped
against the bitter cold, and found Franz

in the teacherage, packing a suitcase.

I stood on the uneven wood step,
                    uncomfortably close to the door,
knocked and stepped back.

I asked if I might come in,
and because of the wind, he had little choice.

"Your parents won't want you to be seen
                    with the likes of me," he began,
and I said I didn't care, that I would go with him,
wherever he was going.

He said, "I'm going back to Saskatoon
where there are other outcasts like me."

I thought he meant other Germans.
Now I'm not so sure.
I pressed him. How am I going to get out of this town
except on the arm of a man?

I wanted to fall to my knees, throw my arms
around his legs, beg and cry if it took that.

He said, "Thanks, but I've already had a run-in
with your father. I'd like to live to see another day,"
his eyes cold as the blue winter sky.

Next afternoon
                I stood on the boardwalk
outside the Mercantile, thinking he'd passed by,
that I could watch him
                        board the train from a distance,
when he strode up, a book in his outstretched hand.

"I found this one you might like.
She was an odd woman, by all accounts —
one Emily Dickinson —
but you may take a liking to it.
I don't much enjoy female poetry."

I held the book to my breast
and watched him board the train.

Jim Loney

Frank came running up our steps three at a time,
bounded into the room while Nora said, "Boys!"
and rolled her eyes.
But she heard Frank announce the news.

"No school until the grown-ups find a new teacher.
No more pencils, no more books! No more
Lahr's dirty looks!" Frank chanted.

He looked around. "Man oh man, have you got it made.
No one to tell you what to do."

I nodded my head sideways, toward Nora,
sitting at the kitchen table, reading the mail.
"Bossy sister," I whispered.

Frank pointed at me, at him, at the door.
We scrambled toward the coat tree.

"Where are you going?" Nora demanded.

"Out."

"Not until you bring in more wood for the stove
so I can cook supper, you don't."

"Do it yourself." Out we went.

"You're gonna pay for that," Frank said, grinning.

Nora Loney

I took Addie with me to pick up the mail.
Nothing from Ran. Not yet. Every time
I ask, "There's nothing else?"
And Carol looks at me like I just insulted her.
"No," she answers, curt and quick.

Turns out Effie hasn't paid the light bill
in four months. One piece of mail
was a notice saying we owe seventeen dollars.

Ran left us eight dollars. I counted
                    our little pile of money
sitting in the middle of our kitchen table
to see what we had left.
Six dollars, forty-four cents.

I shooed Addie out to collect eggs.
He came back with just two in his basket,
tugged me by the arm back outside,
impatient as a child who has to pee
as I re-buttoned my coat and boots.

"Why, oh why can't you just tell me?" I implored him.
But Addie kept his tongue firmly in his mouth.

The chicken house door squealed on its hinges.
Addie shooed Harriet off her nest
and revealed the tin of Papa's drinking money.

Four dollars and fifteen cents.
I hugged him — felt like he'd found
the goose's golden egg.

The other piece of mail was from Danny.

Danny Filmore

Dear Nora,

Well, I am writing to you at last.
They keep us pretty busy in EFTS.
I got here riding the slowest
piss-poor train in Canada, I swear.
On weekends, we have dances. You should see
the girls that show up. They all want to dance
with a guy in uniform.
Of course, I wish they all were you, Nora.

First I got shipped, like every recruit, to Manning Depot.
Manning's where they poke at you
and inoculate you and take your clothes away,
and give you clothes that make you look exactly like
everyone else.
Then they put you through deep knee bends,
running on the spot, marching around the parade grounds,
cleaning latrines
and doing every other joe job you can imagine.
Then you get to eat food that looks the same every day

and sleep in Barrack Block with a hundred other snoring,
freezing bodies.

Then it was ITS, and finally, they sent me here.
And now I'm in pilot training.
Yessirree, Danny Filmore is going to be a pilot.

I've been eyeing those Tiger Moths
ever since I got off the train. So far,
all I get to do is wash the damn things with my bare hands
out on the windy tarmac.
But, I promise you, pretty soon
I'll be pointing the nose of that Moth
right into the clear blue sky.

Big test coming up 0800 tomorrow.
Got to read my manual.
I hope you are thinking of me,

Yours Always,
Dan

Nora Loney

Someone knocked violently on our door.
I opened it. A man in a fedora and black coat
towered over me.
"Ah, so this house *is* inhabited.
Might I have a word with your father,
that is, if he can be inconvenienced
to show his face?"

I said, "My father is not at home."

He said, "Then I need to speak to the lady of the house."
I said, "I am the lady of the house."
He studied me a second, as if to size me up.

Behind him in the yard, Jim and Frank
had scattered their planes over the snow,
Addie doing his level best to kick snow into the air
as flak the planes flew through.
The frigid air curled up into the space beneath my dress,
and my legs stung with cold.

He shook his black-gloved finger at me.
"Look, girly. I'm not here to play games.
Your father owes four months back payment
on his electric bill.
It may come as a complete surprise,
but you have to *pay* for electricity.
I'll return tomorrow to see him."

I said, "He won't be home tomorrow, either."

The boys made bombing noises as only boys can do.
Even from the doorway I could tell there were casualties
littering the snow.

He pointed his finger at me, his thumb straight up,
as though he were holding a pistol.
"Now you see here, girly girl —
I have half a mind to shut off your power right now.
Can you comprehend in that vacant little head of yours
what that means? It means no lights.
It means no radio.
It means no whatever-else-you-have that uses e-lec-tri-city.

You tell your father he needs to have seventeen dollars

to hand to me on Thursday."

He stepped off the porch.
The snow squeaked beneath his boots as he walked away.

Addie Loney

Light man came back.
Found out our papa's dead.
Mama, too.
He was mad.

The grain elevator
poked out of the top
of his hat.

Nora gave him money.
His footprints
keep walking away
in the snow.

Nora Loney

Jim and I had it out
after I sent him to the Mercantile with Addie
to buy two tins of beans,
then to Selemka's butcher shop for three hotdogs.

It should have cost 65 cents.
He came home with those items,
and a handful of penny candy.

Jim said, "What's the big deal? It's a *penny*."
I said, "We have one dollar and forty-four cents.
That's what we had left
after the electric man took five dollars,
and you spent 65 cents on food
and wasted a penny on candy.
You'll wish you had that penny
when this money runs out, buster."

Jim said, "Ran's sending money.
That's why he signed up. To send money home."

I said, "Have you seen any of it yet? If so, show me."

Jim looked at my outstretched palm.
"God, you sound like Effie.
It's coming, okay? Don't be such a battle-ax."
I could have swatted him with my cooking spoon.

I was about to launch into a tirade about how he was now
the man of the family, with responsibilities.
But as I opened my mouth,
Addie began emptying his coat pockets.
A stick of butter. A box of Jell-O. A tin
of tomato soup.

"Man oh man, kid," exclaimed Jim.
"Even I didn't see you do that."

Carol Williams

Geraldine was in here getting her mail,
minding her own business for once in her life,
when Ethel Meany walks up, starts in on that Franz Lahr.
You'd think if a fella'd left town already,
people could stop grinding him up.
Like he was a pencil in a pencil sharpener
and she had hold of the handle.

"Now maybe this town can get back to normal," Ethel said.

If you ask me, Argue's full of crazy people.
Put Argue on skids and slide it over Weyburn way,
could anybody tell the difference between us here
and the mental?

Anywho, Geraldine starts up
on getting a new teacher soon as possible.
"If I have to keep my four boys home longer than a week,
in this weather?
Why, they're going to start prying the doors
right off their hinges!

Oh, by the way ..."
Between the two of them, five minutes hadn't passed
before they'd decided a reasonable fate
for those Loney children.

"Unsupervised children are the Devil's workshop," Ethel said.

George Loney (deceased)

Gawdammit, I still can't get this shape of mine
to do what I want. And Maggie just skims the floor
so graceful, turns and scowls at me.
          I know I'm in the doghouse, but this
not speaking to me except in commands and gestures —
          how long will it go on?

I promised her I'll make amends.
Tonight I hovered in the boys' room,
Addie asleep with that pillow on him,
not under his head. Always slept that way.
Jim with his hands behind his head,
          working out some thought. Jim —
always smarter than me, and I know it still.

Foolish I looked, standing on the bed.
He looked right through me, Jim did.

I called his name. Then he saw me.

Slapped his hands down on the sheets.
Sat up board straight.
Shoved himself against the iron bed frame.
I tried to calm him. What the hell.
Never done this before.

"Son," I told him, "first of all,
I'm sorry I wrecked your fort.
Now I'm on the other side, I can see
it was the best use of beer I can think of. Heh.

Now. I'm sorry I missed your speech
                              at the school that night.

Folks said it was terrific.
'He going to make a good man,' Otto told me.

Rye was my demon, see. It haunted me —
from the time I was seventeen, every moment of my life.
It was my torturer, the claw inside my brain.
It aimed to destroy me.

Anyway, son, what I want to say is
be good to your sister. She needs you.
Work hard. You'll be a good man."

I might have had some other words
but they choked in me.

Jim answered.
"Pop. It's okay, Pop."

Said, "I miss you."

Jim Loney

Got up this morning, sat at the edge of the bed,
wondered if it had been a dream.

I felt wrung out, worn through,
as if heartache could beat you to a pulp,
bruise every last bone in your body.

I ran my fingers through the air
at the end of the bed.
Nothing.
I only ached deeper for Papa,

the pop I'd hardly known,
the gentle, contented papa.

First thing, I went down
and lit the furnace. Then
I lit the stove. Nora
stumbled into a warm kitchen
as I came in the back door
carrying the wood box, full,
kindling already topped up.

I think she was about to hug me.
Didn't think I could take that.

I said, "Fed the chickens.
Off to look for a job,"
and headed out into the frigid day.

Danny Filmore

Dear Nora,

Greetings from SFTS Yorkton!
I've moved up in the world —
            training in the Avril Anson.

By next week I'll have logged all my hours
in the air, night flying included.
            Another daylight solo flight
            and a night solo flight to go.

Then it's Wings Test
and Wings Instrument Test,

then Wings Parade
and I'm on leave for Christmas.
I can't wait to come home and see you.

A number of us guys got to making these
in our spare hours. It's simple, really —
a bit of salvaged Perspex
cut into a heart shape —
polished with button polish,
a small hole drilled to make a pendant,
a miniature in metal and enamel
of the RCAF badge affixed behind.
I thought it looked pretty swift
once I finished it.

For you, to remember me
when I'm flying ops
over Jerryland.
If anything should happen,
I want you to have this from me.

Here's hoping you're keeping warm in this cold.
Do you have a Christmas tree up?

Your Dan

Ran Loney

Dear Nora, Jim, Addie and the chickens,

Do you remember those summer days at the farm,
a thunderstorm over our heads, and all the chickens
rushing into the house?

There we were, riding out the storm
with 40 chickens huddled around the stove.

I thought of that today when our take-off was aborted
by chickens on the tarmac.
The CO is still trying to figure out
how the damned things ended up there.

I hope you've been getting my letters.
I'm sending more money in this one.
I hope that helps you out.

I'm here to tell you, Moose Jaw is the line
where all topography ends.
At least around Argue we have a few hills
and Wood Mountain to the south.
Just north of here there's nothing in your way
until land meets sky in a straight line
all the way around you.
From the air though, it's a sight.
I've seen the world as a bird sees it.
When I die, I want to come back as a bird.

I haven't received any letters from you
so I've written my address clearly on the envelope.
Hope everything's okey-dokey as we used to say.
Would love to get some news from home.

Tell Susanna hi from me.
Tell her to write to me. I miss her
and all of you. Even the chickens.

Your loving brother,
Ran

Mary-Ann Meany

Mother has found my packet of poems —
a few sheets of paper folded and folded,
then cut and stitched to make a primitive book.
I'd hidden it
stashed among the goose down in my pillow.

How she discovered it I don't know.
But there she stood in my bedroom,
my poems in her knotted hands,
a feather nosing its way
from between the pages, open
to this:

The Father

His footsteps in the hall —
Midnight — his feet so deftly fall
upon the wooden floor —
then his hand upon the door –
I felt it as if he'd touched my skin.
His ghostly presence in the room
before me — his blackened form.
I feign sleep. No moon tonight,
no light at all, nor hope of spring —
only crying, only pain.

Mother's lips quivered over her teeth.
Her eyes accused me.
She whispered,
"How could you do this to your father?"

I watched at the top of the cellar stairs
as she descended, opened the furnace door

and tossed the packet in.
The paper flared, curled black and died.

Jim Loney

I started with the Mercantile.
Mr. Argue studied me, said, "Everybody knows
my grandfather founded this town,
                    started this Mercantile,
and everybody knows
I don't take help from anybody.
Hard enough to make a living
what with every person and their dog
from here to Mossbank asking for credit."
He leaned over the counter
            and put his face within an inch of mine,
a little drip from his nose dancing on his moustache.
"And some sly ones slipping stuff into their pockets
and not *paying* for it."

My growling stomach kept me going.
I went next door to Frank's dad's butcher shop.
"Sorry, sonny," Mr. Selemka said.
                    "This job too dangerous for boy like you.
You go cut your fingers off — " He held up
his famous left middle finger,
                    missing the first knuckle.
"I done that when I was fourteen. Older than you."

I thanked him and turned to leave.
                    The bell jingled above the door.

He said, "By the way, how's that dog of yours?"

I shrugged my shoulders. "I got no dog, Mr. Selem — "

"I *said*, 'How's that dog of yours? He hungry?"

"Um, he's fine. My … dog's fine."

"You give him this." He wrapped up a soup bone,
held it across the counter.

"You come tell me when your dog gets hungry."

Susanna Payne

I did it every day this week —
rose from bed, walked out the door of my room
and down the hallway to the bathroom,
my hand on the wall to guide me.

It was a buckle in the carpet runner
that tripped me.
I tumbled to the floor.

Father had not yet disappeared
into his consulting room.
He came running.

"For Godsakes! Would you stop trying to do that?
One of these days you'll break a leg,
or your neck,
and then where will you be? Confined
to a wheelchair for life."

My father retrieved my crutches from my room

and would have pulled me to standing
if I hadn't stood under my own power.
He didn't seem to notice,
                                        or if he did,
did not see fit to encourage me
by acknowledging the fact of my standing
            on my own two unbroken legs.

My father holds me down as if to drown me.
Unbeknownst to him, I have completed my application
to Normal School
                                and have posted it in the mail.
I have a secret advocate — Mrs. Helen Davidson,
my violin teacher. She says a girl like me
should get an education. She says
I could teach school,
            and I could teach violin after school.

I will find a life away from this town.

Jim Loney

I walked into the New Moon Café.
Mr. Lim stood behind the cash register.
Paper lanterns hung from the ceiling,
a framed dollar bill on the wall.

He said, "No. I am sorry. My boy Victor,
maybe he leave for war
when he turn eighteen. Then
I need help."

I turned to leave.

He said, "Hey — we close seven o'clock.
You come, back door."

At Bob Lively's gas station,
Mr. Lively looked me over.
"I don't need a town kid.
What I need is a farm boy
who's used to hard work."

I reminded him I was born on a farm,
and I split wood every day for the stove and furnace.

He said, "So you can use an ax?"
"Yes sir."
"I gotta take the truck up to Wood Mountain,
cut forty or fifty Christmas trees.
Pay you two dollars to go with me to cut trees,
and twenty-five cents for every tree you sell."

I nodded eagerly.

"Bring your ax," he said.

Nora Loney

Dear Dan,

Thank you for the beautiful pendant.
I shall wear it every day.

I'm so proud of you for becoming a pilot.
Please send me a photo of you in uniform.

Jim, Addie and I are making do on our own.
I imagine your mum has told you Effie's left.
Of course, we're fine here,
and we've got the chickens.
If they stop laying in this cold,
we'll have a feast of chicken dinners every night!

Yesterday I told Mr. Childress
not to leave any more milk on the step
as I'm trying to be prudent with money
until Ran sends some along.
I think I'll miss that milk less
than I'll miss Bennie
pulling up with the wagon.
I love those feathered feet
and shy eyes beneath his mane.

We're well and fine.
I've lost a bit of weight even.
Has Ran come to your station?
We haven't yet received word
but we are checking the post every day.

Yes, Christmas is coming. We don't
have a tree up yet, but I'm sure we will,
and it will be festive around here.

Your Nora

Carol Williams

"Is that a new dress? A new department store dress?"
Louise stuck her head through the bars,

both hands holding on
as if she were prisoner in a jail.

"This little thing?" I retorted, still sorting mail into cubbyholes.
"On sale. Hudson's Bay. Regina.
Bargain basement, of course."

I didn't want her to know what I really paid for it.
That's nobody's business but my own,
and the whole world knows what a busybody she is.

"Eloise Roberts says Clara Innes has a new dress.
Wore it last Sunday to church."

She scrunched up her eyes and nose.
It made her whole face look like someone
had taken it in hand and squeezed it for juice.

"If you ask me, those Anglicans
pay their preacher too much.
I guess if they want to see their Sunday offering
turning up next week in Clara's dress,
that's their business.
You'll never catch me setting foot in an Anglican church.
Just one step away from Papists, they are."
She gave her head a nod to make it stick.

"There's all kinds of people in the world," I said.

"By the way." Louise grazed on another tidbit.
"Have you noticed — the Loney girl
wearing a necklace sent from that Filmore boy? I wonder
if his mother knows her son is sweet on a girl
from the wrong side of the tracks?"

Nora Loney

I lit the lantern
                and took Addie with me to the cellar.
We have half a bushel of sprouting potatoes,
half a dozen canning jars of beets,
three jars of carrots,
four of rhubarb,
two of green beans
and six of applesauce,
and about a thousand cobwebs, centipedes,
                                mice and spiders.
The last of our milk sits
in the ice box on the back porch.

Jim was gone until after dark.

Addie and I each ate a hardboiled egg and a potato,
and four spoonfuls of beets each,
and I gave Addie the last cup of milk, warmed,
which he drank with his spoon.

Addie Loney

I saw Papa
beside his chair.
In the window the moon
was singing
and the milk in my spoon
was the moon, and Papa
white like the moon.

Nora Loney

When Jim came home from Wood Mountain,
he brought inside with him the smell of the night
and the sharp scent of pine.

In the kitchen he pulled the money
out of his pocket —
a couple of dollar bills and some quarters,
which he released from his fist onto the table,
the coins spilling like a scattering of stars.

Still he held those one-dollar bills
in his soft boy hands,
folded, the way a man would,
and suddenly I could see the man he would become,
the man who lived in him already.

I didn't notice the burlap sack
until Jim put his hand in and brought out
a soup bone wrapped in paper,
and a container of browned rice.

I put the soup bone in the ice box
but, ravenous, we sat down
and ate every last grain of rice.

Jim Loney

I sold seven Christmas trees door to door,
dragged two at a time over the snow,
and when I sold those two, went back for more.

I figured it was kind of like advertising,
letting folks know that Mr. Lively
was in the Christmas tree business.

No matter how rich or poor they are,
people will pay a dollar for a Christmas tree.

On the way home I passed the New Moon
and remembered to come to the back door,
thinking Mr. Lim might pay me a dime
to sweep the floor.
But he took me into the steamy kitchen
where pots were coming off the stove
and into the sink.
Mr. Lim spooned rice
with pieces of carrot and peas and bits of meat
onto a plate, covered it in tin foil.

I thanked him.
He said, "Bring this plate back."

Nora Loney

I put Addie to bed with a foot warmer
filled with coals from the stove
and wrapped in dishtowels,
then tucked it beneath the quilts.
The other I tucked into the foot of my bed
and set my cold feet against it
and breathed the fierce cold
of our upstairs rooms.

A noise outside brought me alert.

Something in me said *Papa*
            wandering home, *Papa* humming
in the night air, the wind carrying his tune
and the stars winking behind the wind,
and the next moment
would be his sound on the steps,
his hand creaking open the front door.

And just as suddenly, I came back to my senses
and found myself crying, trying not to waken the boys
as memories rushed back
                through the open door of my sadness.

I had measles, I think. Or scarlet fever.
I lay heavy with sleep; my eyes ached with the fever.
The room, dark. Mama
                opened the door
and Dr. Payne rushed in with his black bag,
holding a lantern in front of him.

I remember that light —
but nothing else — except
that I must have slept
and when I woke again,
                Papa was there.

I could hear the air slide in and out of his nostrils.
Papa in a kitchen chair,
his hands folded between his knees.

Papa waiting out the fever with me.

Ran Loney

Dear Nora, Jim and Addie,

Nora, do you remember the time
we were sent home from school with our report cards?

I'm sure you know which report card I'm referring to.
I had a D in History and some other
unremarkable grades.
I stuffed it into a gopher hole on the way home.

Mama made me go back and find it. Too bad
the gophers hadn't chewed it up.

Well, you may be surprised to know my marks
in my flight course:

Airframes	90	Signals	99
Engines	88	Navigation	95
Armament	84	Airmanship	85
		Theory of Flight	94

At any rate, my average was 90.7,
which ends my course.
I'll get my RAF Navigator's Certificate, Second Class,
and my next posting. For most of us,
it will be to Y depot, Halifax. In other words,
overseas.
The money I sent in the last letter
is for rail tickets to my Wings Parade,
December 23rd.
I want all three of you to come
and pin on my wings.

We're having a dance afterwards at Temple Gardens.
We've all booked rooms
          at the Brunswick for the night.

Your letters haven't gotten through —
check the address again.

Say hi to Susanna for me. I've been writing to her
but have received no replies. Is she mad at me?
Or does all the mail for Argue
get lost in gopher holes?

Believe you me, getting no mail from home
          is a piss-poor thing when everybody else
is opening up perfumed paper from sweethearts,
packages of tobacco and socks, etc.

Your loving brother,
Ran

Danny Filmore

Three days to Christmas break.
I had my final solo flight in the Anson,
took off on a clear afternoon, CAVU conditions —
          Ceiling and Visibility Unlimited —
headed out of SFTS Yorkton for SFTS Regina.

Colder than hell frozen over, even
in that flying greenhouse, as we call the Anson.

                    But the sky — robin's egg blue,
the roar of the engine filling my head.

I was happy as a pig in a poke up there
until I looked down —
          nothing beneath me
                    but a dirty blanket of cloud.
Snowstorm had moved in below me.

I began descent. But the ground was gone.
We had been lectured on the dangers
          of letting down in these conditions.
I reached across for the envelope of emergency maps.
There was none.

I put the aircraft into a shallow spiral descent
and pressed my face into the window
to peer downward. Nothing but white.

Suddenly a dark shape off my port wing —
                                        a grain elevator.
I leveled off at 50 feet above ground,
circled the elevator to buy time,
caught sight of the airport fence, then whiteout.
I'd have to set the kite down
in a crosswind.

Who knew I wasn't the only one
                    setting down in that storm?

I don't remember the crash.
I heard no explosion. A flash seared my eyes.

I hung in the air over the wreckage
unaffected by the gale force winds,
                                   the stinging snow,
watched emergency personnel
          point their fire hoses on the flaming metal

quickly coated in ice, peered
onto my charred remains and thought,
Dammit.
I wanted to be home for Christmas.

Nora Loney

I was boiling clothes in the washtub
on the stove, rubbing my knuckles raw
on the scrubbing board,
listening to Glenn Miller on the CBC
when I jumped at the sound
of a pounding on the door.

John Argue held Jim and Addie
by the coat collar, one in each fist.
He dragged them inside the house
without letting either go.
Beside him stood Constable Fortin, RCMP.

Jim said, "I'm very sorry, Mr. Argue. Sir.
I swear I didn't see him do that."

Mr. Argue leered at me. "Did you know, Little Miss,
that your cretin has been *stealing* from me?"
At that moment
he threw both boys to the floor
and produced the goods he'd pulled
from Addie's pockets.

Constable Fortin stood over us
as Mr. Argue demanded Addie be arrested.
I held Addie to me, stared both of them down,

as much Mama as I could muster, and said,
"How in heaven's name can you arrest a seven-year-old child?"

We paid Mr. Argue inflated prices for his goods,
listened to him carry on about how Addie
belonged at Weyburn.

"Addie is not leaving my side."
I looked them both in the eyes,
as if to dare them.
Both men left
when we agreed Addie was never
to enter the Mercantile again.

Frank Selemka

I took our day-old newspaper over to Jim's.
We lay on the floor and read the comics together —
"Tippy and Capp Stubbs," then "Diversions."
I read out loud —
"Farmer Harlo Hansen of Stockton, California,
couldn't put up electric fence around his stockyard,
as a calf ate the instructions."

Then a knock at the door. Electric man.
He wanted twelve dollars to keep their lights on.
Nora offered him a dollar fifty-seven,
said it was all they had.
"JesusMaryandJoseph," the electric man said,
and stomped off.

We were halfway into the radio show,
Are You a Missing Heir?

when the radio man's voice quit.
Lights went out.
                    We sat in the dark
as Nora stumbled around for a lamp and matches.

"What do we do now?" Nora asked,
                    setting the lamp on the floor.

But we never came up with an answer.
Down the road, there was a scream.

We ran to the door and looked out.
Under her porch light was Irma Filmore
with a telegram in her hand.

Jim Loney

Mr. Lively closed his tree lot at sunset,
let me take home the last scraggy tree.
                              I dragged it behind me,
shook the snow off on our front porch,
opened the door and hauled it in.

Nora sat at the kitchen table
                    staring into thin air,
muffins cooling on the table,
one hand at her necklace,
her voice like dust
          carried off in a wind
when she opened her mouth.

"I spent seventy cents on flour
and baking powder —

used the eggs we collected
yesterday —
half a jar of applesauce."

Then she looked up at me, but didn't seem
                    to see the tree.
"I thought we should take
something over —
I thought ...
it would be ...
nice ..."

"Yeah, sure — " I started to say,
when someone knocked on the door.

It was Jack Fletcher with a telegram.

Nora's eyes bugged out. "No ... no ..." she choked.
I opened it.

Coming home for Christmas. Meet train at 1400. Love Ran.

Margaret Loney

Now I skim the snow behind you, Nora,
                    down the white road,
you carrying that pan of muffins under cloth,
your pitiful offering.

Grief holds your jaw taut,
my boys scuffling beside you, heads down
toward the Filmore house, studying
how their worn-out shoes shake off snow.

Nora, honey, hear that hall clock chime
as you raise your fist
                    to the knocker on the door.
Don't listen
to the drivel that will blubber
                    from Ethel Meany's mouth.

Oh! If you could only see me behind her
mimicking her every movement,
while my boys eat like ravenous birds!

Nora Loney

The Filmore house was filled with people,
mostly Catholics, but Meanys were there
                          with Mary-Ann,
as well as Father Innes and Mrs. Innes and Adam.

The kitchen was piled with food —
Catholic food and Anglican food —
and the Presbyterian church circle ladies
in the middle of it, washing dishes, drying
and setting them out again.

Mrs. Filmore took our gift,
thanked us from behind her drawn face,
and Ethel Meany immediately
                    lifted it from her hands,
ripped off the tea towel. There they sat on the dining table,
slouched and forlorn: my little muffins.

Mrs. Filmore admonished us to eat —
                          Please, please, eat this food —

and Jim and Addie readily obliged.

Mr. Filmore sat in a chair in a corner
and stared at nothing.
Father Innes placed a hand on his knee.
"Ned," I heard him say.
"How can we best help you, Ned?"
But Mr. Filmore was in some far-off place.

Then Father Innes patted his knee and stood,
when, all of a sudden, Mr. Filmore seemed to awaken,
looked up at him and cried, "If you want to do something,
bring my boy back!
Make my son alive again!
Go perform a miracle
with your broken bread and your ridiculous little cups!"

The room stilled with the echo of his words.

Slowly, the conversations began again.
Ethel Meany then cornered me —
behind her I could see Jim and Addie
filling their plates a third time —
looked down her hooked nose at me
and said, "Some people have no business
being here. This isn't a restaurant
where you and your hobo brothers
can sit down and gorge yourselves.
Daniel Filmore was a hero.
The last thing Ned and Irma need
is a Jezebel like you around."

Stung, I slipped on my coat and left quietly,
closing the front door softly as I could.
But Father Innes opened the door

almost as soon as I had shut it.

He caught me, placed his gentle hand on my shoulder.
I hardly dared look into his blue eyes
as he said, "This is a difficult time
even if you're not one of the family ..."

And left me then to walk home,
fire the stove to warm the frigid house.
I sat watching the wood take the flame
and could think only, in that moment,
of the weight of his hand on my shoulder,
how suddenly I wanted him to be my father,
and I a child again.

George Loney

I held myself down with magnificent effort
to the kitchen table — as close
                              as I could get to Nora
sitting there on a box with her face in her hands.

I didn't want to frighten her, so I spoke softly,
"Close the door, sweetheart."

Her head jerked up. She saw me
in my ungraceful position. I thought
the first words out of her mouth might be,
"Don't stand with your feet on the table,"
but her mouth just hung open.

"Close the stove-box door, honey.
                                        Let it heat up the room."

Did as she was told.
Always was a real sensible girl.

"Nora … you know I always
hated to see a woman cry, how I'd follow your mother
around the house, try to say
the right thing. You know how that turned out.
Maggie waving her hands in the air,
crying louder and louder.
Hell, I'm sorry, honey, for every gawdam thing
I failed at.
But I've given up the drink … "

Gawdammit, what a stupid thing to say —

"Look — my hands don't shake now — look
how steady they are …"

Hell, George, can't you come up with anything better
to tell your daughter than that?

"Look, honey. It's not just love … this father business …
it's duty … just as much as love.
I flunked duty, that's the God's truth.
I guess I just want to say …"
Shit. I don't know what to say.

In death as in life.
Couldn't say the right thing to a woman
if my life depended on it.

Jim Loney

Me and Addie were the most enthusiastic eaters
at Filmores, at least until Frank arrived.
At the end, Mrs. Filmore packed up a ton of food,
said, "I noticed you boys really enjoyed that.
Why don't you take it home?"

The look on Nora's face when we brought it all
into the kitchen — I couldn't tell
if she was embarrassed or relieved.

I thought she'd be hungry. Instead
she made us save it all for Ran.

I went out to the chicken coop,
down to the cellar, out to the shed,
found three kerosene lanterns.
                    We trimmed the wicks,
filled them halfway.
That way, all three lanterns got some.
I hung one off the lamp
        over the kitchen table.

Then we put up the tree, brought out the ornaments —
the paper chains, our baby handprints
                    in paint on newsprint,
Mama's glass crêche.
It was quiet without the radio,
                        but then Addie
wound up the gramophone,
put on *The Pearl Fishers*.

Next day, Christmas Eve,
was the longest day in history, I swear.

Nora wouldn't let us eat the food
she was saving for Ran.

I had the brilliant idea
that we should go to every church service
in town, so we could eat.
Nora agreed, but made us dress up.
I almost regretted the whole thing.

Four and a half hours — count 'em — in my wool suit.
The Presbyterians had butter tarts,
shortbread and tea.
The Anglicans had sausage and cheese balls
and little meatballs you stabbed with toothpicks,
butter tarts, shortbread and tea.
I figured they'd better have real food
after all that flipping through the prayer book.

The Catholics were best of all —
we had to stay up for midnight mass
and couldn't understand a thing they said,
but afterwards they had a ham, Ann Gabb's buns,
sausage rolls, stuffed cabbage, deviled eggs,
cookies and tea.

Addie and I stuffed as many of those buns
into our pockets as we could.
They'd be a little crushed for Christmas dinner,
but who cared?

We opened our front door about one in the morning,
and it was frigid cold, of course. Nora
wanted me to stoke the furnace hopper,
but I told her we were low on coal.
I'd wanted to find another time to tell her this,

that we were going to have to haul our beds
into the kitchen to sleep around the stove,
to save on wood and coal.

Nora declared it wouldn't be until Ran
had come and gone.

Addie Loney

The train hooted like an owl.
I rode on Ran's shoulders
all the way home.

I was a bird up there
in the middle of the sky.

Ran Loney

I walked to the station from the Brunswick Hotel,
a hangover raging in my head and gut.

Tossed my duffel into the baggage net,
fell into my seat and closed my eyes.

I didn't know whether to be angry or worried
that no one bothered to write or send a package
or come to my Wings ceremony.

I slept, opened my eyes
                                        at Assiniboia,
where I could see the southern hills at last,

round and barren against the sky,
a hawk flying so high it caught the sunlight
          and shone like a spark,
and knew I was nearly home.

We pulled into the Argue station,
the grain elevators welcoming me
with their roofs tipped with snow,
wind lifting the snow to look like hair
on their ridiculous heads, then
the open door, the smell of siding,
                              the platform,
my sister and brothers
looking more grown than I remembered,
more ragged.

First thing we all said to each other was,
Why didn't you write?

Nora Loney

I got up early on Christmas morning,
                long before the lazy dawn,
took the lamp out to the hen house,
picked two hens that hadn't been laying —
Tess and Frieda.

Spent all morning cleaning them
to put in the oven for dinner.

We didn't have any presents,
but we had Ran, whole and handsome
in his uniform, his wings pinned

above his breast pocket.

I wanted to hang onto him,
touch his shirt, his arm, his face,
just to prove he was home.

He was angry about the money
never reaching us.
I felt somehow responsible,
and apologized,
which caused him
to lash out at me, and of course,
stupidly, I cried.

He spent three hours with Susanna
and I was jealous of the time.

On Boxing Day Ran slept in,
spent the morning in the Mercantile,
afternoon and evening at the Buffalo,
regaling every man in town
and more than a few of the women, too,
with stories of his training.
He was the star of Argue
and seemed to love every minute.

Next morning we put him back
on the train, Addie
riding his shoulders again
as far as the platform.

When he turned to say goodbye,
I was sure he saw the terror in my face,
that I saw Danny's fate in him, too.
We grasped his hands

through the window,
and the engineer blew the whistle,
and black smoke fell over us,
and the train jerked forward, squealed,
and left us behind.

Carol Williams

Louise Gillingham walked into the Mercantile
for sugar and oats, took note in her way,
that makes everything sound like a complaint,
that it was cold back here.

"My Queen heater's on the fritz," I said.
"Got to get the government to buy me another one.
Lord knows I can't afford to get it myself."

Louise never was what you'd call
a heavy thinker.
I figure I can just about look through her forehead
and see what she's going to say. Usually
I'm right.

And I was. Nothing in this town is nobody's business.
"Well, *I* heard
you got a new electric range for Christmas.
When are you going to invite me over
                    to get a peek at it?"

And, "You *do* know, don't you, about Mary-Ann Meany?"
As if she knows more about Argue's goings-on than I do.

Just because I'm Anglican doesn't mean

I don't know what the Presbyterians are doing.
She talked like I was a foreigner just parachuted into town.

"Ethel's worried about her. She was sick all over Christmas.
Still can't keep a thing down, Ethel says.
They're taking her up to Regina today — city doctor.

Ooh! Is that a new brooch you're wearing?
Don't tell me that's a *real* pearl!
From some distant relative?"

I just hummed. "Umhumh." It can mean
anything you want it to mean.

Dr. John Payne

Two days after Christmas, Ethel Meany
brought her daughter to my consulting room.
She'd been retching and vomiting for a week.
        No fever. No chills.
Lungs clear. Lymph nodes normal.
Tonsils not inflamed.

I tossed the tongue depressor into the trash,
turned toward the two of them, said,
"When my wife had symptoms such as these,
        she was pregnant with Susanna."

I'm a doctor, not a preacher.
It's not my job to tell them what they want to hear.

As they left, Ethel's face formed into one
        mountainous accusation;

Mary-Ann hunched like a caged bird.

I washed my hands and retreated
into the house, where Susanna
methodically moved between dresser drawer
and suitcase,
pulling out a blouse or nightgown, carefully
refolding it into its new home, all
while balancing tentatively on her two feet,
that is, without crutches.

I agreed to send Susanna to the teachers' college.
What could I do but let her go?
I could never stand against
that single-mindedness,
a trait she inherited from her mother.

What she sees as resistance in me
is my fear
of what I will become without her —

an old man who waits out the night
after Mrs. Gabb has shut the door behind her.
Indeed, a forgotten man
who will measure out the hours of darkness and silence
in a cavernous house
filled with furniture and china and musty air,

the remnants of his lifelong success.

Susanna Payne

Ran surprised me with his visit.
He claimed he'd written, swore
he'd sent gifts — a little pin,
a pendant, a photograph of him in uniform.

Oh, how I wanted to believe!
He sat there on the red velvet chesterfield
so sincerely, gentlemanly in the uniform
he thought I'd be proud to see him in.
He drank tea, balanced cup, saucer
and a square of shortbread on his lap.

I decided I didn't care if he'd lied or told the truth
as he'd come of his own accord to see me,
and that was enough.

I told him of my acceptance
to Normal School, Moose Jaw.
When he wrote from England, I said,
Father would bring his letter to me,
and then I would reply with my address,

though I didn't expect any letter
once he was exposed to those English girls
with their pretty little accents.

I walked slowly, hesitantly about.
He seemed impressed with my awkwardness,
and when he left at last, we clasped hands tightly
and said our goodbyes.

I wanted to throw my arms around his waist,
bury my face in the smell of his shirt

so that I would never forget it,
but young men can promise many things
and I couldn't help but think
Ran Loney could have any girl he wanted.

What could he possibly want with a cripple like me?

Ran Loney

Quite a lot can happen
on one miniscule spot of land.
Argue's always been that way.

An insignificant cluster of houses,
a few stores and other wood structures —
from the perspective of a kite
it's even more puny.
And beyond, the prairie grasses
poking out of snow,
and of course wind
busily turning back to brown
a white field or road
beneath the blue face of the sky.

I tried to hide my anger about the lack
of mail from Susanna, the pin
I'd specially picked out for her, lost —
a little fan of gold plate, a pearl
at its base — and wanted to see it
gracing her graceful neck.

She was as I remembered,
delicate as a bird,

the waves of her blonde hair
framing her green eyes.

I confess, piss it all, to a lightning strike of envy
as she told me of her plans.
Once that girl is steady on her feet,
every serviceman in the city of Moose Jaw
will be asking her to dance.

And so I didn't kiss her goodbye
or hold her fiercely as I wanted,
the dreaded thought that already
she was growing apart from me
sharp in my mind.

From the deck of this ship
I look across a prairie of sea and wonder
what will happen to us now.

V

The Schoolteacher

Mary-Ann Meany

Father drove the Buick. Mother
                    sat silent
in the front seat beside him.
I could see in the window's reflection
her pursed lips, the lines
around her mouth, each
a reprimand, each
an accusation.

I rode in the back seat
like a child on a journey
to visit grandparents, only
without a doll to occupy me,
or puppy to keep me company.

I had dressed against the cold
but not against that other cold
of my mother and father.
How did Father know
where to take me?
My minister father
should not have knowledge
of these things.

It was a shabby house.
We parked three blocks away
and entered at the back.

They kept me there over a night
after they'd scraped the baby out
and let me bleed until I stopped.

Something in me died, too,
in that place.

When they returned for me at last,
I wore a stone face
and eyes of glass.

Jim Loney

I took the enamel pail
and filled it from the little pile of coal
in the cellar. I won't miss
going down there — spider webs,
smell of mice droppings,
and bumpy plaster spread over damp earth,
and dark corners where zombies
could be lurking,
                    just waiting to grab you.

I set the pail by the kitchen stove
and then we took the bed apart
and hauled it downstairs.

When I complained to Nora
that we'd had nothing but pancakes
since Ran left — pancakes and rhubarb,
pancakes and applesauce,
pancakes and chopped beets —
she declared that it was time

I went hunting.

"If we kill and eat every hen
we'll have no eggs to eat,
no eggs to sell come spring, no chicks.
You have to. You're the man."

Ran Loney

Dear Nora, Jim, Addie and Chickens (minus Tess and Frieda),

Well here I am in jolly old England.
Everything green here, but wet —
a cold that goes right through you.
I've been forced into my woollies.

Can't tell you where I'm stationed —
they'd just cut it out, anyway —
but I'm happy here,
tho' everything is bloody expensive
and the only writing papers we can get
are these airgraph forms. I was lucky
to grab the last one.

I'm plenty ready to get back into the air,
as I've been grounded so long
I feel as if I'll take root pretty soon.

Met some of my air crew today.
Bill Harries, an Englishman from Lancashire,
is absolutely the wittiest fellow I ever met
and one hell of a nice guy.

Then there's Nigel, our flight engineer,
and our bomb aimer, Gord Hicks, an Aussie,
who must hold the world record
for being a wolf.
Everything strictly above board, but watch out
soon as he sees a skirt.

And Jake our tail gunner —
from Medicine Hat, for Christsakes.
First thing he does is take out a photo of his girl,
and don't you know she's the plainest thing you ever saw,
and he says, "Ain't she pretty?"

We all get serious and nod our heads.
"Yep. She's, *ahem*, pretty alright,"
and Jake starts in about how his girl's expecting,
how he plans to marry her when he gets home.

Now Jake doesn't look as old as me even.
So Gord the Aussie pipes up and says,
"God stone the crows, cobber!
So you knocked up your Sheila, and she'll
be your trouble and strife —
ding dong, barstud!"
And Gord slaps him on the back so hard,
nearly knocks the breath right out of the poor fella.

Half of my chums are sending money home,
as much as $20 a month. I know
that would help you out a lot,
so I've signed the forms
to send it directly.

I've been working like a pisser these days
doing cross-country and a lot of flight planning.

That took up my daytime,
and then we had night flying.

But we had half a day off last week
so we went to a little town near here
and met the nicest little old lady.
We had a good chat, the five of us fellas
in my squadron,
and she ended up kissing us all goodbye.

Turned out her son had trained in Canada
and to hear her tell it, folks treated him like a king,
so she wanted to return the favor.

That's about all for now.
There isn't piss happening around here
except for some WAAF dances,
                    and I don't much care for them.
Never meet any wavy-haired blonde girls who play the violin.

Say hi to Susanna for me,
that is if I don't get my hands on
                    another airgraph form soon,
and give her one of these pictures of me.
I know they're all ghastly and really can't fathom
why Bill's camera didn't break from the strain.

Your loving brother,
Ran

Gideon Freeman

I'm out early in the morning. Yes.
Want to be down in the wolf willow
when first light breaks in the sky.

That's where I get my rabbits.
It's what I mostly eat in winter.
Umhumh.

I was hunkered down out there
waiting on a bit o' light
when Jim Loney shows up
making all kinds of noise,
snapping twigs, stumbling
through brush.

Had his brother's Cooey .22,
decent rifle for a youngster,
but any rabbit worth his ears
coulda heard him coming.

Look, I said. Look for their tooth marks
where they chew on the wolf willow.
They like young trees best.
Now, you be on the lookout
for that rabbit's eye —
                    when he blinks.
Sometimes that's all
the movement you'll see. That's right.

Now ol' Mr. Rabbit sits tight in his cover.
Then he'll get flighty
if the hunter stops, and then
he might just break from the underbrush,

and that's your chance.

I showed him and I showed him
how to give that rabbit plenty o' lead
                                    and follow through.

Now, that Jim Loney's a right smart boy,
but if he don't learn quick
them children ain' gonna have
no meat on the table. No sir.

Mary-Ann Meany

Father presided like a king, as usual,
over his Sunday morning flock,
preached on the coming of the Wise Men,
said we must give our very best selves to Jesus,
sang, *On Christ the solid rock I stand,*
                              all other ground is sinking sand,
as he walked back up the aisle in his purple robe.

I stayed home from church, watched
from my bedroom window
                              the chosen come and go,
wondered, how do you get to be one of them,
               and not one like me?
                              Is it God who decides?

It's a sin to stay home from church,
Father says. He says,
"If you miss church because your ox
                                             falls in the ditch,
either get yourself a new ox

or else fill in the ditch."

Neither Mother nor Father seemed to think it a sin
to keep me home today.
                    They don't want anyone to see
          the circles under my eyes,
my hollow stare, the fire of my anger
that has taken flame
somewhere deep within me.

It wasn't even a week
since they drove me to Regina,
yet Father crept into my room
          late last night.
I felt him before I saw him there.

I rose from bed screaming,
took hold of my desk chair,
                    held it in front of me.
Its legs stuck out like some stiffened animal.

I screamed, "GET OUT! GET OUT
          AND LEAVE ME ALONE!"

Mother came running, flipped on the light
which shone harsh upon us, and said,
"We do not raise our voices
in this house, young lady."

Jim Loney

A rabbit sure cleans up easier than a chicken,
slips right out of its skin.

The chickens eat the entrails,
and I can sell the pelt at the Hide & Fur.

Nora was so happy to see two rabbits
hanging from my hands,
I didn't have the heart to tell her
Freeman shot them, not me.

But I went out before sunrise again.
What's so hard about shooting a rabbit for food?

I stepped through the brush, checked
for teeth marks on the saplings I passed.

In the gray light I saw an eye,
then white fur, a winter hare.
I watched its quick breath,
its sides in and out, in and out.
We watched each other and together
breathed the frozen air.

I whispered to it, "Rabbit,
I love your soft fur, your little tail.
I marvel at the power in your hind feet.
I see the fear of me in your eye.
I promise, when I am no longer hungry
I will never hunt again."

He broke and ran. I aimed ahead of him,
followed through just like Freeman said.
Heard the pop, felt the rifle kick back,
saw that hare go down.

I ran to pick up the body,
eyes that no longer saw me.

Out of nowhere I could see, Ed Childress
stood over the bleeding hare.
Pointed his old Enfield at me.

"This here's my rabbit. Keep
your grubby little paws off my rabbit."

George Loney

I keep thinking I need to pack a bag or something.
I guess the dead travel real light.
I followed Addie out back,
watched him toss grain to the hens, then
gather the eggs in his quiet way,
his little hand around each one.

I said, "Addie, son, you see me here?
It's your old man."

And that little guy looked at me
like nothing out of the ordinary,
nothing at all. He grinned,
held up his basket of eggs.

"Yep, I see 'em, son."
I like to encourage the little fella.

"I just want to say
I know I should have let Margaret
                    take you to a doctor or something,
someone who could figure out why you don't talk.
Well, I just shoulda done that.
I'm sorry I never did.

Now, I know Nora and Jim
would be real pleased if you
could start saying stuff to them —
                    using words and such.
I gotta go on a little trip, son,
but I hope you find a way
to get those words out.

I'd be real proud if you did."

Ran Loney

G'day, mates, as Gord says to us
every goddamn morning.

We just had leave and then changed stations
and I can't tell you where we are, of course,
but the same RCAF Overseas address will do.

Well, fuck a sad duck if I didn't run into Howard Selemka
                                        my first night here.
He gave me this pen as my old one gave out.
He's been assigned to my flight crew,
so that will make seven of us.

I haven't received any mail from Argue,
but I hope at least the money is getting through,
as I know dear Jim will eat every morsel of food in the house
and the tablecloth for dessert.

Good news — the supply of liquor here is quite good.
I've been here four nights and have been drunk two,
                                so that's not bad.

On arrival we received our 218 Squadron's badge.
It's an hourglass with the sand
almost run through.
Good omen, don't you think?

Our first flights were in four-engined Halifax bombers
to get us accustomed to the feel of the heavy bombers.
I've also continued my training in map reading
and passed my night vision test.

We're supposed to be flying the new kites soon — Stirlings.
Jim, the Stirling's wing span is just 99 feet
to allow it to fit inside standard RAF hangars.
So when you carve some Stirlings, remember that.
Just don't let your Messerschmitts take us down.

Your loving brother,
Ran

Margaret Loney

The children carried the boys' bed into the kitchen
to sleep by the stove, rely on cordwood,
let the rest of the house go cold,
the last of the coal reduced to ash.

Even short on cordwood.
Why George never cut enough
to last the winter, I never knew.
Always, always. Every blessed year.

Now I watch my Jim and my Addie
scour telephone poles, scrape off

large slivers with their pocketknives
for kindling,
walk the railroad tracks
for fallen wheat and scattered
lumps of coal.

Nora's boiling clothes on the stove,
hanging them in the kitchen
on my winter line. Both Addie and Jim
have such holes in their trousers
they'll have to wear both pairs at once
just to keep covered.

I never wanted this for my children.
Of course I didn't. Why, oh, why,
when the doctor lays that new baby,
all bloodied and fussing
on a mother's belly, the cord
still attached and pulsing,
she believes, if only for a moment,
the world will grow kinder
simply because she birthed a child?

We mothers are blinded by love,
and love it is that makes me suffer now.
I consoled myself by sitting in the rocker,
set the gramophone's needle on "Je crois entendre encore,"
from *The Pearl Fishers.*
Nora, abruptly,
stopped her stirring of the clothes,
walked into this cold parlor, spoon in hand,
saw only the needle's nodding head, and my chair
blindly rocking back and forth.

Mr. Lim

Somebody knock, back door.
Those two boys.

My wife pack food for them.
Bowl of soup. *Lo mein.*

The new teacher, she sit, over there —
out of the wind when the door open —
soup, and tea,
she write in a little book.
Her glasses slip down like this —
middle of her nose.

Ruth Parker, Schoolteacher

I arrived by train from Manitoba,
said my goodbye to trees, ponds,
the gentle curve of the land.
It was a fierce wind greeted me,
and that sky —
the only thing growing in this season.

But I had seen, just out of town,
a creek, frozen hard, a puny grove
of trees and brush,
and I thought that small stand
just might save me here.

And I was shown to my quarters:
two rooms, a table
that would serve

for meals, desk and bookshelf,
stove, sink,
a bedroom well named
as it holds scarcely more
than a bed
and my trunk.

And I was shown the school —
sturdy and sufficient, then
was told I could take my supper
at the New Moon,
where I drank soup and tea
and Mr. Lim
would not let me pay.

And I noticed two young boys
ushered in by the kitchen door
who looked for all the world
like street urchins
in Dickens' *Oliver Twist*,
or the prostitute's son
in Harte's *The Idyl of Red Gulch*.

I reminded myself then
what my professor father
would say to me:

Even if they are, Ruth Parker,
even if they are,
that's none of your business.

Addie Loney

We sleep in the kitchen now.
Flowers on our windows.

Nora Loney

I blew out the kerosene lamp
and we climbed into bed. Our kitchen bed.
Jim on one side, me on the other
and Addie in the middle.
We lay staring at the ceiling
as though it were a night sky
filled with stars.

I said to Jim, "Remember the farmhouse?"
And Jim said he used to lie in this bed,
hearing Ike and Nell
stamping and snorting in the barn.

Wood popped and cracked in the stove,
Jim talking about the farm.
"Back then," he said,
"when the dust was everywhere,
do you remember that? The dust?

Papa sent me and Ran out
to bring in the stooked wheat
for threshing,
with Nell, Ike and the wagon,
and we were coming back along
the section-line road when it blew.

The dust came up
so bad, couldn't see the road.
We had to trust Ike and Nell
to know the way.
And out of a ditch already
filled up with dust
rose up some dark, huge thing.
I thought it was an animal.

It was Ned Filmore.
We hauled him up to the seat.
All of us looking like bandits
with our shirts over our noses.
I slid back and rode
in the wagon box with the wheat.

Ran drove the team real slow,
and I remember thinking, 'Hey, the wind's stopped.'
I felt our wheels bump
over the railroad tracks.
I looked up. The locomotive,
gigantic, black,
loomed over me, its lamp
dim, like the moon behind a cloud.
Maybe five seconds we had
before it would have hit us.

See, after the wind stopped, the dust
just hung in the air, and you could hear
no sound at all. Not a thing."

Addie was asleep.
Then Jim nodded off,
as though telling that story
relieved some part of his mind.

I lay on my back a long time
feeling that locomotive
in its silence, over us.

Jim Loney

That weasel's hungry
just like us.
Digs under the chicken wire
and goes straight for the eggs.
What eggs we had
the weasel mostly got for himself,
and skittish hens don't lay.

Sounds like a chicken alarm clock,
all that clucking and squealing
and bashing wings. When
he can't get eggs,
he'll strike like a snake,
grab one by the neck
with his needle teeth,
haul it under the fence and across the snow.

I told Nora we're losing inventory fast.
She looked at me like I'd told her,
Guess what, the world is round.

But she made me go out anyway
and kill another hen.
I grabbed Mabel by the neck,
stared into her beady eye and said,
"Sorry, Mabel. I really hate
to do this to you."

This is how you kill a chicken,
if you're not a weasel.
Stuff its body under your arm
to keep the wings from beating you to death.
Hold onto the feet
if you don't want to get clawed to death.

With the other hand, take hold of the neck
and let go of the feet. Swing it over your head
until you hear the neck pop and crack.

I brought her in to Nora. She held Mabel by the feet
and dunked her into scalding water.
Jiggled her up and down to get the feathers off.

I was just trying to distract us
from our dwindling supply of poultry
when I said,
"Do you know who holds
the world record for chicken plucking?"

Nora looked at me
like I was speaking some ancient language.
I answered, "Ernest Hausen,
Fort Atkinson, Wisconsin, 1939,
plucked a chicken in 4.4 seconds."

Addie jumped up and down.
Nora stayed quiet, those scaly chicken feet
in her fist, dangling it over the pot.
Then she said,
"Do you have an encyclopedia inside your head?"

Nora Loney

Every day before I can ask,
"Is there any mail?"
Carol turns her back to me,
says, "Not today, honey,"
and sounds like she's speaking to a child.

I left the Mercantile quickly,
felt my face grow red, as though
I'd been rebuked. Almost missed
Mr. Selemka's brisk knock
on the window of his butcher shop.

He waved me in.
"How's that dog?" he asked,
and I've learned to say, "My dog's fine."
And he handed me a soup bone
wrapped in brown paper.
I took it from his big hand,
the middle finger missing its end.

On my way home I saw Miss Parker
walk into our yard. First thing
to catch her eye was Jim
breaking up a bedroom door
for firewood.

I could hear plain as day
Mama's voice in my head, saying,
"For goodness sakes, dear,
invite her in for tea."
So I did.
She picked her way around the bed
to sit at our kitchen table.

I had no fresh-baked bread,
no muffins, butter or jam.
As soon as Jim came in with wood
I would put Mr. Selemka's soup bone
in the pot and boil it with our last
potato and a turnip,
and that would be our dinner
for as many meals as it would make.

Already she seemed to know about us.
"Why, you must be Addie," she said
when he peered around my skirt
and flapped his hands like a bird
about to take flight.

Ruth Parker

I knocked on every door in Argue
and introduced myself,
whether or not there were children
in the house.
Every other person seemed to need
to warn me
about the ragamuffin clan
living fatherless and motherless
in that tumbledown house at the edge of town.
One or two even assured me
that should I decide that Loney child
needed to be at the Mental,
they'd see to it he got there.

Ice crystals bloomed in intricate patterns
on the windows.

Frost collected in the corners
of the unused rooms and on the walls
like a fresh layer of whitewash.
One bed in front of the stove.
A kerosene lantern over the table.

The children have not washed for some time.
Perhaps it is due to the lack of stove wood,
as I saw the elder boy breaking up
a door in the yard.

The young lady advised me
                    it might be difficult
to persuade her brother to attend school.
The boy came in bearing a wood box full
with the remains of the door, then sat down
and drank weak tea with us.

He looked at me askance,
asked, did I know about Pluto —
                    the planet, that is.

"Indeed I do," I said.

Ran Loney

Dear Chaps,

I've been in England long enough it seems
I'm getting to be more and more a Limey
all the time.
          We're at a new station —
one hell of a nice one, with a blessed good mess

and the prettiest WAAFS I've ever seen,
the kind that makes strong men weak
and weak men weaker.

You'll never guess — ran into Milt Meany.
He was on his 12th ops already
by the time I arrived.
We had a hell of a time together the other night —
had about a gallon of beer each.
My dinner left with the last of the gallon
but we thoroughly hashed over old times
and I even made it back to my bunk
under my own steam
before I passed out.

I'm with the same crew and here
they have a picture show six nights a week
which Gord, the Aussie, bloody likes a lot.

Our first night was Gardening Expedition —
dropping a few landmines
in the Bay of Biscay.
Next night we were up on the board
for a raid over Emden.
Halfway over, 18,000 feet,
our pilot Bill announced we'd lost power
in the port inner engine. Bill circled back.
We jettisoned some fuel and several bombs,
but set the kite down, still 3,000 pounds overweight
and on three engines to boot.

I can't complain as we are all fine
and could be worse
as we're missing seven Stirlings that haven't returned.

Milt's crew limped in, too,
the tail shot nearly all to hell.

I'm sure it will be old news by the time you get this.

I was there when they washed Milt out of the turret
with a hose.
I went off and had a roaring drunk after that.
Don't know who I felt sorrier for — Milt or myself.

Anyway, I'm not getting any of your letters
and am still wondering why the hell I never get mail.

Has Susanna gone to Moose Jaw?
I'll try writing there.

Hope they find a schoolteacher brave enough
to settle in Argue.
They'd better not tell her or him
what tough customers you are.

Your loving brother,
Ran

Mary-Ann Meany

My mother and father talked late into the night.

In the morning, Mother carried a suitcase
into my room, filled it
with my few possessions,
said I wouldn't need
my best dress and shoes.

I watched, expressionless.
It is too much effort now
to contort my face
into happiness or sadness.

I dressed when I was told to dress.

My father opened the car door for me
and shut it after me. He drove east
as the wind blew the snow away,
as though someone had thrown off a sheet,
and underneath lay the land — naked, brown.

Along the wide boulevard
just outside Weyburn,
the black branches of trees scratched at the sky.
The hundred barred windows stared
unblinking, ahead.

We climbed the steps, entered
the domed-ceiling room and stood,
hands folded as if in prayer,
as though we had made this pilgrimage
to make ourselves holy,
cleansed from sin.

There they checked me in.
A nurse with a ring of keys at her waist
took me by the elbow and led me away.

Here I would remain until such time
as they might come back for me.

Carol Williams

Agnes and Louise were flapping their gums
at my window when Jack Fletcher
swaggered up, telegram in his hand.

Louise said, "Who's that telegram for?"
And Jack, not being the sharpest nail in the bin,
said, "I can't tell you. It's government property."
Then in his next breath he says, "Where's
Reverend and Mrs. Meany?
They're not at home. Looks like their car's gone."

As if three clucking hens
can't put two and two together.
I offered to keep it for him, said
I'd give it to Ethel and Albert
soon as I saw them drive up.
I'd make sure, I said.

"I'm not allowed to deliver this
to anyone but the addressed recipients,"
says Jack, "and if you've got a notion
to make me go against regulations,
you ladies have got another think coming."

I could see Agnes behind him
rocking her head from side to side,
as if to say, *Well, la-di-da.*

Jack left with the telegram still in his hand,
though we tried our darndest to weasel it out of him
without going so far as to pry his fingers apart.

After he left, Louise says, "Ethel told *me*

they were driving their Mary-Ann to college
at Radville. That Bible college there."

And Agnes gives Louise her best withering look,
as if Agnes has got the real news and that ain't it.

"What Ann Gabb told me was
Ethel brought her Mary-Ann
to see the doctor right after Christmas,
          and the doctor
mentioned to Ann that the girl
          had a bun in the oven,
and it was that Franz Lahr put it there."

I said, "Imagine — bringing shame down
on a respectable family like that."

Ran Loney

Dear Addie, Jim and Nora (in ascending order),

Well, I've about had enough of this rain.
I would gladly trade it for some nice cold, dry snow.
Jim, are you hunting any rabbits?
I should have thought to take you for a run-through
                    on Christmas Day,
though I suspect any of the frozen chosen of Argue
would have strung us up for shooting hares
on the day of the Lord's blessed birth.

We've made seven tours of Jerryland etc.
and really blasted the hell out of them,
but I have to say you wouldn't recognize this crew

after they've climbed out of the kite
and headed off to the pub.

Well, it was a good thing
no officers were there drinking last night.
Bill does a helluva job of imitating our CO —
I swear he must be the funniest bugger I've ever met.
You'd never know, if you only knew him in the kite,
what a kid actually resides in that six-foot frame.

Anyway, we're on ops tonight,
so we don't get to see Bob Hope in *Road to Zanzibar.*
Lunch was fried eggs and bacon, and beer.
Nigel, our flight engineer, thinks this *Tirpitz* run
could be a shaky do.

Only twenty-three more ops to go.

Father Andrew Innes

There are rumors spreading over the party line
about Mary-Ann Meany being with child, all
while Albert and Ethel are grieving
the loss of their son.

Of course, nearly everyone in town
went to the Meany home,
bringing what people bring in such circumstances —
food, and more food, as some murmured
over why Mary-Ann had not returned
after news of her brother's death.

Ethel, bless her soul, was for the most part

without words.
Albert preached, because even
when one has no words,
a man of the cloth can quickly
pull out chapter and verse
in place of deep feeling.

In the midst of this, the Loney children
have begun to attend my parish, much
to the dismay of some of my parishioners.
My guess is
that they go to Albert's church at ten,
ours at eleven.

Clara and I sat up into the night last night
discussing the issue of the children.
Ragged, cold and hungry,
they sit out the service, apparently without energy
even to fidget, then pocket
whatever is placed on the table at coffee hour.

The reading for the day was Mark 5: 21-43,
the story of the unclean woman who dared
to touch Jesus' robes,
and by her faith was healed.

I read the gospel passage in the center aisle
among the people, as is customary,
then climbed the steps to the pulpit
and took a deep breath.
"The compassion of God,"
I told my flock, "doesn't ask our permission. It does not abide
by what we decide is clean or unclean.

After all, why has Jesus come, if not

to seek out and save the lost?
Whom do we exclude from the grace of God?
Who needs to be brought in from the cold,
from the edges of life,
who needs to be loved?"

After the service, Otis Stoughton said
the prayer books were in bad shape
and needed to be replaced.

Edwina Scott mentioned the Loney children,
reminded me that their parents had never
been on this church's rolls,
had given not a cent to this parish.

Addie Loney

Mrs. Innes is going to give us
music lessons.
Nora argued
because we don't have any money.

Mrs. Innes has a
net on her hat.
Her hat is shiny
and I want to touch it.

Jim Loney

Sunday night, Nora made us wash.
Just like a sister, she ignored me

when I told them both not to watch
while I bathed in the galvanized tub
we dragged into the kitchen.
But Nora made us both go stand in the parlor
when she bathed.

Next morning she checked our hands,
under our fingernails, behind our ears.
Watered down our hair, combed over our combing.

Frank knocked on our door. We took off ahead
of Nora and Addie, our cigar box of planes
under my arm. Frank picked up pebbles
in the dry spots of the road where the wind
had worn the snow away, chucked them
at magpies and a rabbit
sunning itself beside the tracks.

The older boys had gone up the night before
and strung fishing line all over the room,
from one desk top to another, so they'd fly open,
to books on the shelf so the books would tumble out,
to the ring at the base of the pull-down map
so it would flap down
like a great big tongue.

We had to crawl to our desks.
We waited for Miss Parker to come.

Ruth Parker

I believe in ignoring bad behavior,
long as it doesn't get out of hand.

And so when I saw that the classroom
had been booby-trapped, so to speak,
I ignored it. As my sister Kate
always said, "Ruthie, you can keep
that face of yours slack
even in the darndest situations."

I took attendance. I learned names.
I asked who would go home for lunch
and who would stay.
When the Loney children
didn't raise their hands
for either choice,
I ignored that, too,
though Victor Lim, a polite young man
whose family runs the New Moon,
stood up and seemed to feel the need
to inform me in a booming voice
that they were "charity cases."

Just to look at them one could see
their bones, their eyes dark and sunken.
A desperation about them.

Nora hung her head, her face
gone hot and red
as the chilblains on her hands.

As for the waste of good fishing line,
I suppose it wasn't a waste if the joke
was good, but I let the books tumble
from the shelves,
the map open its giant mouth
and roll back again, and made
no comment whatsoever.

I would clean it up
after all were dismissed.

For the morning's final hour,
I read to them from "The Luck of Roaring Camp,"
a tale of gold prospectors who,
                                        saddled with a baby,
clean up the town, put up curtains,
wash and change diapers — a ragged bunch
of unlikely mothers.
You could have heard a pin drop as I read.

I had planned ahead for the Loney children,
brought sandwiches and hot cocoa
for their dinner, gave Jim the job
of coming early to stoke the stove
and sweep the floor each morning
for 15 cents a day.

There had come a warming wind, a chinook
that took much of the snow away,
leaving quite a bit of dry ground,
with the exception of a particularly
large mound of snow at second basc.
I'd found a bat and ball
but no gloves. We could make do,

and played softball all the afternoon.
Four teams playing alternate innings,
and I the umpire.

It was a good first day.

VI

France

Margaret Loney

I heard footsteps on the front porch,
a knock at the door. Jack Fletcher,
what do you want with us?

I followed him back down the road in the wind,
the billowing dust, but could not tear
the telegram from his hand.

I skimmed the road back home,
cranked up the gramophone
to *Madame Butterfly*'s final scene,
rocked and wrung my hands
all the afternoon.

I watched the road
until I saw Jack leave for coffee
at the New Moon.

            The telegram
sat on his desk, addressed
to George and me.

I whisked it home.

Ran Loney

We got the forecast before takeoff:
high altitude cloud. A cover.
Instead we flew into a crystal clear night
and a full moon.

The Jerries had only to find the vapor trail
and follow it to the bomber at the other end.
Whatever anyone says about the Jerries,
they aren't stupid.

We had no warning. Jerries
approached from rear and below —
                                        our blind zone.
Ammo ripped into the starboard wing
and right side of the fuselage.
Several of us hit by flak.
We lost all control. The kite
began to plunge from the sky.

The smell of burning fuel
turned my stomach. Bill
gave orders to bail out.
I grabbed my chute,
                          lifted the escape hatch
located just under my table,
the others already in line,
waiting to drop.

I dropped through,
was jerked around mightily
                                        when my chute opened.
Stunned by the intense cold,
I began to swing below the chute

in a circle, like the swing ride
at summer carnivals.

Nora Loney

A telegram lay on the floor
just inside the front door.

It was Jim finally ripped into it.

CP Telegraphs
R.C.A.F. Casualties Officer
February 2, 1942

Mr. and Mrs. G. Loney, Argue.

Regret to advise that your son R two five three three two five eight Sergeant Randall George Loney is reported missing after air operations overseas January twenty-ninth. Letter follows.

R.C.A.F. Casualties Officer

We stood stunned
          for some minutes
until Jim moved
to collect firewood.

Nothing to eat,
and not even Jim
          asking after food.

We undressed and climbed

into bed in the dark.
When I was certain the boys
were sleeping,
            I covered my face
with my hands, and cried.

George Loney

I slid into that Stirling bomber
                        just in time for takeoff.
"You stick by our boy," my Maggie said to me
with that look in her eye.

What a way to fight a war.
                        Who said this crap
is better than trenches and shit?
These kids are just flying targets
was the first thing that came to, well,
            what's left of my mind —
but dammit, I was right.

Shrapnel flying everywhere, fire
in the fuselage, bombs still on board.
Whose idea was this?

Seven crew. I counted four
that got out before that rattle-trap
exploded in mid-air.

The air warmed as I followed Ran down.
That tree came up fast, slashed him bad
across the face, but he held. Unconscious.

Then the sound of boots on the ground,
voices barking commands. Ran
jerked awake, hung up in the tree.
Had the good sense to stay quiet
until the noises died away.

After a bit, he released his harness,
scrambled down branch by branch,
hit the ground and collapsed.
I stood over him. Wasn't a thing
I could do.

Good God, son, here you are in Germany
without boots.
Nothing but your stocking feet.

Ran Loney

I felt a wetness on my face
and wiped my sleeve across it.
Holy shit, I heard myself say out loud.
My sleeve was covered in blood.
And I was not prepared to be lost in Europe
without boots,
knocked off somewhere between bailing
out of the kite and landing in the tree.

My socks already worn through in spots,
I turned them over
and walked on the tops of them.
I looked to the stars to gain my bearings
and proceeded west, more or less,
until I'd need to find cover

once the sun came up.

I then started down a gentle slope
toward a creek, and found, not too far ahead,
it fell sharply
into a cut in the earth. I found a space,
a low overhang, and crawled in.

The ground was damp, but after scooping up
branches and brown grass I made a nest,
then ventured over to the creek.
Washed my face.
My wound stung with the cold.

I opened my escape kit and took stock
of what I had. Several chocolate bars.
Packages of soup concentrate.

Halazone tablets to purify water.
Rubber water bottle.
Benzedrine tablets — bennies —
to keep me going in an emergency.
French, Dutch, Belgian money.
French-English dictionary.
Matches, compass, maps.

Under my little overhang I spread out
the map of western Germany
and located my position.
From time to time I heard voices.
Kept still.

But it was cold, wet,
not like the dry cold of home,
and I didn't know what it would take
to keep me warm.

Ruth Parker

Jim and his sister and brother
arrived as usual at seven o'clock
to stoke the stove and sweep the floors.
All three of the children helped out,
and I had to tell them
I couldn't pay all three.

I suspect they simply wanted to be
someplace warm.
I heat up cocoa for them when they come.
At least I know they've that in their stomachs.

It was not quite noon,
the younger children busily
drawing maps of their town. Jim
has begun reading my set
of *The Book of Knowledge*
and is now on the second volume.

I was teaching the few remaining older boys
the science of flight, the geography of war —
anything to hold their interest
and keep them in school,
though I've lost every young lad I had
over the age of sixteen,
and know the enlistment office would take
my fifteen-year-olds
quick as a wink,
without a second glance.

And then the butcher arrived
asking for his son, Frank.
A bright boy, that one.

Frank left his seat and returned shortly
to collect his books, his coat.

"What is it, Frank?" I asked.

"We got a telegram," Frank answered quietly.

We sat dumbly as his boots
scraped the floor.
No one, neither the little children
nor the big restless boys,
made a sound.

We sat for many minutes in that silence,
as though a blanket had been draped over us all,
until I rose
and dismissed us for the day.

But the Loney children remained.
I brought them to my teacherage,
fed them soup and bread.
They ate in silence
until, rising to take their leave, Jim said,
"We got a telegram, too."

"When?" I asked.

"Two days ago."

They had told no one.

Carol Williams

Damn. I didn't know it would be this.
All these envelopes look alike. I can't deliver this now
in the condition it's in.

February 11, 1942

Dear Mr. and Mrs. Loney,

I am writing to offer my sincere sympathies in the anxiety you have experienced since learning that your son, Sgt. Loney, R.G., is missing from air operations.

He was the navigator of an aircraft which took off to operate against the enemy on the night of 29/30 January 1942, and the aircraft failed to return. Nothing has since been heard of it or of any of the crew.

There is a possibility that your son may have escaped the aircraft by parachute, or in a forced landing in enemy territory, in which case he would be a Prisoner of War. The International Red Cross would be first to receive any such news, and they would pass it immediately to Air Ministry, who would communicate with you as per your son's situation.

I feel most deeply for you in this difficult time. We all join with you in hoping and praying that your son is safe.

Very Sincerely,
H.J. Smythe
Wing Commander, Commanding
No. 214 (White Cliffs) Squadron

Ran Loney

I could see when I pressed my sleeve
to the slash across my face,
it still bled. I made
a poultice of mud and slapped it on,
hoped it would dry and close the wound.

Soon I found I couldn't walk far on railroad tracks
or even roads with much gravel on them
for the rocks tearing into my already bruised
and blistered feet.

I altered my route to travel cross country.
The snow cushioned my journey
until it turned to slush, and then,
as frosting on the cake, it rained.
My feet went numb and stayed that way.
From time to time
the stars showed themselves
enough to give direction,
but the mud added weight to my socks.

The countryside was dotted
with small three-sided sheds
filled with bundled branches.
I stumbled upon one
and crawled to the back wall
behind the piles of branches.

For a time the sun came out
and heated the wall behind me.
My body warmed. My clothing
began to steam and dry.
Feeling well hidden at last,

I rested my head against the wall
and slept.

Mary-Ann Meany

I walk these halls in silence —
my visitor — the sun —
pass each angelic congregant
in the church of the misbegotten.
Someone moans an organ tune —
another sings a hymn.
We break our bread, exiled, condemned
for what we have not done.

I am not unhappy here.
It is a kind of monastic life.
The doctors and nurses for the most part
leave me alone. I have even made a few friends,
and four or five of us meet each week
to read each other our poems.

And I am free here. I no longer
live in fear.
I am not told what to believe
or what God thinks of me.

No one burns my little hand-sewn books
in the furnace fire.

Nora Loney

That weasel came back this morning,
chased our last three hens out of the hen house
where he tried for one, then another.

Jim woke, too, at the commotion
and got into his boots,
the rifle loaded and cocked.
Seemed he spent a good long while
aiming at that weasel
going around and around
like he was chasing his tail.

Suddenly, a crack,
and Jim on his backside in the snow.

I yelled, "Jim! Jim!"
He looked up
at me standing on the back porch,
then at the weasel
bloodying the snow.

Addie Loney

Jim shot the weasel.
He was white
like burned wood
with smoke
at the end of him.

Gideon Freeman

I been aiming for that weasel
for some time now.
                I figured
if I could shoot the little troublemaker,
it wouldn't be no skin off'n anybody's nose,
and I could tan his pretty little hide.

'Twas a cold, cold morning
after that January thaw.
Ol' Man Winter done set in again
          with his white eye.
But I had my eye
          on that weasel's skin.

Well, I heard a rustling about
over't the Loney place,
them chickens kicking up a racket.
So I got my gun out.

Was lifting it to sight
when the shot rang out.

That boy done a right fine job.
Took that weasel fair and square.

Ran Loney

I woke at sunset, found
a jute bag, then another,
which I tied to my feet over my socks.

I chewed a soup cube, washed it down
with creek water and then
decided on dessert: a chocolate bar.
Only five left.

I ate the chocolate as slowly
as my stomach would let me,
            and remembered suddenly
how Howard and I
used to go into the Mercantile
                        to buy chocolate bars
after we'd got our penny payout
for the gopher tails we'd snared.
I could even smell the Mercantile's
                              creosote floor.

I imagined then Nora and Jim and Addie
opening a telegram, not knowing
            if I'm dead or alive,
and Howard's family doing the same.

I couldn't remember whether I saw
Howard bail out of the kite,
or Gord, or Bill or Nigel,
or our tail gunner, Jake.

I stumbled toward a creek
to refill my rubber bottle,
            my mind on my buddies,
and didn't see a young girl
leading three calves to water.

She saw me before I saw her.
For one long moment we stared at each other.
I must have been a fright.

She was blonde, pure and simply beautiful,
but I was sure she'd go home and tell
about the bedraggled soldier she'd seen,
feet wrapped in bags, face
smeared with mud.

As casually as I could,
I dipped my bottle in the creek
                    and pressed on.
I took a benny and went on as far
as it would take me.

George Loney

I had to get that boy some boots.
I spotted a garbage dump
behind a village about half a day's walk
from here, been nudging him
                    in that direction.
The kid's nearly delirious.
He went and devoured the rest
of the chocolate bars
and now he's got plenty o' nothin',
as we used to say on the farm.

The garbage dump was risky,
but the boy found some boots.
Not as good as I'd hoped —
                    holes in the soles,
and one with the sole loose,
but I dropped some wire in his path
and he picked it right up.
Good kid.

Getting that lad across the Belgian border,
now that was something else.
That border guard hadn't a thing to do
but twiddle his thumbs.
I made noise under the bridge.
Broke some branches,
made the sound
                                        of someone walking.

Ran limped over the bridge
while the guard was underneath,
                                                            searching
for whoever was making that sound.
Broke another branch behind the guy
as he headed back to his post.
That delayed him a bit,
and Ran slipped into the darkness.

Food, now. That's a problem.

Ruth Parker

The Negro man, Mr. Freeman,
paid a visit to my teacherage,
                        a good-sized hare
slung over his shoulder.

I accepted his gift.
We had tea and sugar cookies —
my sister Kate's recipe.

He'd come to ask if I had any books
                                                                        he might read.

He had never heard of Mr. Mark Twain's
Huckleberry Finn.

I started him on that one.

Ran Loney

Felt like someone was following me.
I turned around. Nothing.
Nobody. Still,
it felt like somebody was right on my shoulder.

The boots worked for a while,
and I covered some ground
but then they began to hurt my feet.
Once I found a safe spot
to spend the day,
I realized my left foot was so swollen,
the boot could not come off.

And somehow, I'd lost my compass.

Late in the afternoon it snowed again.
By nightfall I had walked for some time
through snow,
a cold wind blowing off the North Sea.
My swollen foot was so painful
I could only limp along.
The right sole come loose again,
the wire slipped off.
I had to step high with that foot
and lay it down on the flapping sole.

I never actually knew what hungry was,
even when we were scraping along
on the farm those last years.
I spent considerable time
thinking of what we ate then,
each garden vegetable Mama put into jars,
each fat slice of fresh bread,
still warm, slathered with butter.

Finally I looked up, and through the falling snow
loomed something vague, large and dark.
A barn.
I stumbled into a stall, fell into dry straw,
and slept.

It was barely dawn when I awakened
to the sound of voices
and the clang of milk pails.

I thought, *This is it.*
            I was Jerry bait
limping across Belgium like this.

I stood weakly, leaning heavily
on the boards of the stall,
and jerked forward on my painful feet.

A boy, about Addie's age, and a man.

I rehearsed the words in my head,
                        then spoke:
Aviateur Canadien. J'ai faim et fatigué.

George Loney

What the hell happened
to your compass, son?
                    Gawdammit,
I can't keep track of everything.

I knew it was a gamble
sending you to that barn.

But the daughter
looked just like Nora.

Ran Loney

The man and boy helped me into the house,
where a woman and a girl
who looked like a young Nora
laid me on a chesterfield, took off
my wet clothes and covered me
in a blanket.

The man cut off my boot
and little Nora began to wash my feet.
When she'd finished,
she disappeared into the kitchen
and returned again with the basin
filled with clean water.
She washed my face.

They brought out clean nightclothes
and a bowl of warm milk with bread in it.
Then young Nora helped me into a bed

in a warm room.

It was night when the mother woke me,
another bowl of bread and milk
in her hands,
and civilian clothes over her arm.
After I dressed in them,
she forced some shoes onto my feet
and led me back to the barn.

Nearly dawn.
They would need to hide me
for the day.

Someone had made a makeshift bed
for me high in the hay,
where I remained, left to think
how I was placing this family
in grave danger.

The girl and boy climbed the ladder
and peeked shyly at me.
Whenever I grinned,
their heads disappeared.
Finally I remembered the only French rhyme
I ever retained in school:
Un, deux, trois, quatre, cinq, six, sept,
violette bicyclette.

I sang it over and over
until their eyes appeared,
then their noses,
then their giggling mouths.

Before long they sat

beside me on the straw ticking
            and sang with me
until their mother ran out
with a wooden spoon in her hand,
frantically gesturing
to shush us up.

God, I was homesick
at that moment.

Addie Loney

Father Dominic
knocked on our door.

He had a sack
that looked bumpy,
like there might be kittens
in it.

It was clothes.
I wanted kittens.

Margaret Loney

Father Dominic came to the door
bearing a burlap sack
                of clothing
from the St. Vincent de Paul bin.

Granted, both boys have unmendable holes

in their trousers, their sweaters,
and perhaps something will fit them,
some bit of moth-eaten wool
to keep the wind out,
but Nora's face went red
as the setting sun.

She'll not want to be seen
in Susanna Payne's cast-off dresses,
or Clara Innes's,
or our postmistress's, Carol Williams,
who happens to be filling her barns
with earthly goods,
and not exactly putting up treasure
in heaven, if you get my drift.

Dr. John Payne

Mrs. Gabb answered the knock at the door.
I was finishing my coffee, thinking
about whether I would drive or take a train
to visit my Susanna in Moose Jaw.
It was young Frank Selemka,
sent over to collect me.

Ned Filmore had collapsed while shoveling snow.

We carried him into the house,
Frank, Jim Loney and I.
Laid him on the bed.

The Filmore house was positively cluttered
with photographs of their dead son.

A person couldn't turn around in any room
without bumping into a picture of that boy.

I returned to my office,
entered Ned's condition into my records:
Cerebrovascular Accident.
Patient has lost significant movement
on the left side of his body.

But it was grief that felled Ned.
Purely and simply, grief.

Margaret Loney

I skim this house — the walls, floors white
with frost.
And even if I couldn't pass
through doors in my state,
I certainly could now.
Jim's bucked them all up for firewood.
It's a good thing my children's bed
is iron, not oak.
And the Lord Jesus bless their souls,
they haven't got the heart to break up my gramophone.

I stand with my children in the kitchen
as that solid, steady, four-legged table
that was my mother's, that held up
her Bible all these years,
is fed to the stove, consumed
in such a little while.
And how cold the room once it is gone!

Now Nora's declaring one of you
must quit school,
        go to work, bring some money in.
I see you arguing with Jim,
        and you're right, honey,
as much as Jim wants to see that schoolhouse
over his shoulder, he won't go back
if you let him leave it.
                You will.
That's why you must be the one.

And I know just where you'll find work, too,
where that elm tree stands in the yard,
dark as a cloud in the middle of day.

Ran Loney

Someone arrived after dark
            to speak with me.
His English was not much better than my French,
but even I understood the word *dangereux*.

The man came on a bicycle, and somehow
produced another bicycle
on which I was to follow
            at a distance.

I thanked my hosts, hugged those kids
and set off into the night.

I was to watch for his signal.
He would light a cigarette, then
drop the box in front of the house

where I would be taken in.

I swear he smoked so many cigarettes
I was sure I'd missed his signal.

But there it was, the cigarette box
on the ground in front of the gate
to a humble farmhouse.

I walked my bicycle to the door
and knocked.

Nora Loney

Mrs. Meany loomed over me all day
to make sure I dusted her furniture just so,
washed and dried the dishes just so,
and was careful not to knock the plates together
while putting them away. I'd pay
for any chip or crack, she warned me.

I managed a glance out the window
                                        over the sink
as my hands buried themselves in soapy water,
watched the school doors fly open
and the students gather into teams for softball.

But I had little time for my own sadness.
Soon as I had finished the dinner dishes,
Mrs. Meany set me to making the evening meal.
My utter lack of knowledge
about how to use an electric range
convinced her I was a primitive heathen.

Declaring that if I had any faith in God
we wouldn't be poor,
she assigned me to memorize
the Twenty-third Psalm,
and held in her hand a Bible opened to the page,
as though I couldn't find it myself.

Perhaps it was impudence that made me
stand before her and begin,
even before she could place it in my hands:
The Lord is my Shepherd; I shall not want.
He maketh me to lie down in green pastures,
He leadeth me beside the still waters;
He restoreth my soul …

"That's quite enough, young lady,"
she interrupted, shut the book,
and left me alone the rest of the day.

Ran Loney

Again I was hidden in a hayloft
but was comfortable, out of the icy rain.
There was a woman and a man
and a grown daughter
who brought me thin soup
with a few bits of meat floating in it.
I was grateful.

They examined my feet and shook their heads.
When they left me alone, I slept.

I stayed in the loft the next day

and into the night,
the girl returning
with soup and bread,
and the man climbing into the loft
with a pair of socks and three pairs of boots.

I was thrilled to have socks
without holes, and wondered
if they were his own best pair.
I pulled on the boots
and found one pair that fit fairly well.

I smiled, shook his hand, but wondered why
they would endanger themselves in this way
just for a kid from Saskatchewan.

Was awakened near dusk
by the sound of a vehicle.
Peeked out of a knot-hole
to see a jeep
full of Jerries in gray helmets.

And there I was with my boots off.
I slammed my feet into the boots,
my fingers fumbling at the ties.
Already Jerries in the house
and the woman speaking in loud tones.

I took off for the trees fast as I could run. Then,
sudden,
a gunshot, behind me.

Ruth Parker

I looked out my little window this morning
and could see the cold had broken.
Overnight there'd been a change.

Snow still clung to one side
of the fence posts bordering the field
                    across the road —
posts that looked for all the world
like white-haired prophets
                              in the Bible.

I washed my dish, wiped clean
my table, pulled on my overcoat
and walked next door to school,
where I received the news from Jim.

I was so disheartened over losing Nora
that I spent the last hour of the morning
reading Mr. Steinbeck's *The Red Pony*
                    aloud to the class,
and the afternoon beneath a cloudless sky,
in a softball game on the still-frozen ground.

The wind whipped all about us, raw,
but by the shouts of the children
you'd have thought truly it was spring.

Carol Williams

Geraldine marched through the Mercantile
to my cage, both hands raised in the air

as though she were the teacher commanding silence.

"Ooh! Another new dress?
You must have the best job in town, my dear!"
Geraldine was quiet for the merest second.

Then, like a church organ getting pumped,
she started again.

"That Nora Loney's working for Meanys."
She declared it as though it were secret information
known only to her.
"I knew that girl would never amount to a hill o' beans.
Have you seen those children?
Filthy, they are.
It isn't Christian or sanitary to ..."

Just then, Otto Selemka strode into the Mercantile
with a paper in his hand. He spoke
as though a large crowd had gathered.

"We get a telegram," Otto said. "Our son Howard,
he is in POW camp. He is alive."

Ran Loney

I was back on my own,
without food, traveling at night,
vowed I'd not put another family
in danger again.

I figured it'd been about a month
since I parachuted out of the kite.

I left the cover of trees after two days
and began to follow a minor road
when I ran into a Jerry convoy,
their narrow slot lights shining
in the night. I hit the ditch,
and by lying low just missed
the range of their headlights.
But I had to lie in several inches of water
                    until they passed,
and emerged soaked and cold.

I walked all night to keep warm
and by dawn began to search
in fields and vegetable gardens
for moldy cabbage, a mushy turnip.
I retreated to the brush
                    to make my shelter
and eat what I had stolen,
but in the end I tossed it all up
like a kid who's had too much candy.

Nora Loney

I washed the sheets, wrung them out,
hung them to dry. Ironed them.
Mrs. Meany insisted her pillowcases
must be creased just so.

Meat on the table every night.
Two vegetables. Such extravagance.

But they allowed me to eat, too,
and I ate ravenously,

wondering if my brothers
darkened the back door
of the New Moon each night;
wondering if Ran were alive
somewhere and, if I could keep him alive
                                        in my mind,
would he come home to us?

Ran Loney

My stomach was still turned inside out
but something in my head
thought I should keep moving.

Though it was morning I got up,
found a road and continued
on my way.

After an hour I could see
I was coming to a village.
I decided to take the straight route
through town.

No one seemed to pay me any mind,
and I might, if I was lucky,
                grab a bun or two
cooling in a bakery window.

Suddenly a dozen rowdy Jerries
poured out of a pub and onto the street.
Scared the shit out of me.

A man rode by on a bicycle, eyeing me.

I felt him behind me,
and he passed me again
                    in the other direction.

He stopped, lit a cigarette.
As I approached, he said in perfect English,
                                        "Follow me."
I followed at a distance
as he rode slowly up a hill,
then dismounting, walked his bike
into the woods.

I entered the trees,
adjusted my eyes to the darkness.

"I know by your gait you are not
                    one of us.
You swing your arms by your sides, not
in front of you, elbows bent."

I was plenty relieved
that those Jerries
had been too drunk to notice.

He told me of the impossibility
of crossing into France.
He would find someone to take me in.

Remembering my vow, but before
          I could protest, he said,
"Wait here. Someone will bring food,"
and he and his bicycle were gone.

Within an hour two boys arrived
with half a boiled chicken,

a fist-sized hunk of black bread,
                    a bottle of beer
and news that someone
would come to take me to shelter.

Soon the boys returned, agitated,
speaking rapid French,
their wild gestures telling me to get going, fast.

As I moved deeper into the forest
I could hear a convoy on the road.
I kept moving quickly as I could,
                              stopping when I had to,
to vomit up the contents of my stomach.

George Loney

Dammit, son, I even put the beer
          in those boys' hands, the kind
I figured you'd like.

Each night I fold myself around you,
                    try to listen for you
while you sleep.

I do what I can do.

Jim Loney

Who said crime doesn't pay?
With Nora sleeping warm

at Meanys, 'cause Mr. Meany
said his wife needs a live-in maid,
Addie and I make the rounds,
snatch cordwood from people's sheds.

Man oh man we're quiet, not
taking too much
            from any one woodpile,
careful not to step in the snow.
The bare and frozen ground
                        won't give us away.

Nora saves whatever she can
from the Meanys' dinners.
Sets it on their back step,
and Addie, silent as a snail,
            fetches it,
brings it home.

I tiptoed over to Freeman's back porch
where he hangs his rabbits,
gutted, frozen and dangling from a wire.
I just lifted one off.
It cooked up real nice.

Gideon Freeman

I sat beside my woodstove
reading the book Miss Parker lent to me,
when a shadow crossed the page.

Looked up, and by the light of the moon
noticed the shape o' that Loney boy

lifting one o' my hares off the wire.

I reckoned I could keep them kids honest
by setting a bit o' wood and a hare
on their back step mornings.

Addie Loney

In the morning
I find Nora
in the kitchen window
at Meanys.

She brings me a cup
of porridge.
I leave it empty
on the step.

Ruth Parker

I stepped out onto my front step
in the frigid morning for but a moment,
to take a closer look at what
        I thought to be a crocus
peeking out from the crusted snow
still enduring, tough as ice,
        at the base of my house.

Indeed it was — a shock of violet color
and the thinnest line of orange.
Satisfied, I started back indoors.

That persnickety latch
caught me — the door had locked.
I never did receive a key for the door,
and there I stood in my slippers,
my flannel nightdress.

I had just concluded that I must
make a run for the schoolhouse when
Addie Loney slipped around the corner,
silent as a wraith.

"Oh, my! You startled me, Addie!"
I said to him, my hand spread at my chest.
"Now, I need you to go to the back window.
Push that window up. Push it hard.
Climb through the window and come
open this door for me."

The lad did just as he was told.
I watched the door open.
And there was Addie smiling up at me.

While I took a basin of hot water to the tub,
added the cold, I could hear Addie
setting out cups and saucers.
When I emerged — warmed,
washed and dressed,
he had heated water for tea,
toasted bread and spread it with jam.

I sent him to find his brother Jim.
We had the nicest little tea party.

And then we walked next door to school.

Ran Loney

I found a bit of shelter near a creek,
fixed it up with branches,
crawled in and lay down,
my knees close to my chest.

I lay there a few days and nights,
unsure how much time had passed,
delirious some of the time,
moaning at the pain in my gut.

If anyone had come near
I would have crawled out with my hands up.
Surrender must be better than this.

Nora Loney

Mrs. Meany never told me
when I would be paid.
I was told only that I would sleep
          in Mary-Ann's room.
The chilblains on my hands
began to heal.

I lived there little more than a week
when I was awakened in the night.

The light of the moon through my window
                                        betrayed him.

When he slipped into my small bed,
a gasp

escaped from my throat.
My heart pounded in my chest.
I could hardly breathe.

I lay with the wall on one side of me,
with him on the other.
I felt his icy hand
slide beneath my nightdress.
I felt him
touch my breasts. First one,
then the other.
I felt his fingers slide down and down.

In one movement I threw the covers aside,
leapt over him, hit the floor,
knocked a chair aside
while throwing open the bedroom door,
and bolted from the house.

I ran barefoot through the streets of Argue,
terrified he was running after me.

Margaret Loney

That *man* —
I can think of other names for him —
he had placed a chair
at Nora's bedroom door
to stop her in her tracks
should she try to flee,
the chair back tilted and caught
beneath the door knob.

I removed it.

Father Andrew Innes

Our Adam suffered all night with fever
                and a racking cough.
I had sent Clara to bed, exhausted,
and sat praying beside my son
in his fevered state,

when I lifted my head and saw
in moonlight, outside the window,
                a slip of a girl
running through town
in her nightgown, barefoot. Even
from a distance I knew
the expression on her face
was of terror.

I went out then into the night,
braced against the cold.
She ran straight in my direction.
I caught her in my arms.

I understood, even before I opened the door
to walk into the cold,
I had a choice. And I knew

as I carried her to her house, cradled in my arms,
left her in the care of her brothers
and returned home, alone,

at least one person in Argue, Saskatchewan,
                would see me
carrying a young woman through town
clad only in her nightgown.

Nora Loney

I wanted Father Innes to stay with us
and knew he would not.
I slipped into bed beside Addie,
the sheets cold as snow,
though a fire smoldered in the stove.

I thought Jim was asleep.
"Nora," he whispered, and startled me.
I didn't answer.

"Nora," he whispered again.
"What happened?"

"Shut up and go to sleep."

"Nora."

"What?"

"Are you back for good?"

"Yeah. I'm back for good."

"Nora."

"What?"

"We missed you."

"I missed you, too."

I shivered through the night,
listening for Reverend Meany's shoes

on the porch steps,
his icy hand on my breast
frozen in my mind,
and was sure I had not slept.

But in the morning
I saw someone had hung a young hare
from the eave
            of our back porch
and set a neat stack of firewood
below it.

Father Andrew Innes

I confess after carrying Nora home,
I came to church next morning
without a sermon —
            the one I'd prepared
seeming wholly unsuitable for the moment.

I sat through the first hymns and prayers
wondering if God would give me anything to say.

At the appointed time I stood in the pulpit
and opened my mouth.

"I have to say I have never understood
all these theories about how Christ
                    atoned for sin.
But I have had enough evidence
from the goodness of people,
and from what I perceive to be
            the goodness of God,

to keep going.

We have a choice.
Evil and suffering can paralyze us,
or we can take it upon ourselves
and transform it into a greater good.
It is up to each and every one of us
to make that choice.

The ministry of Jesus is not about
wanting God to verify our presumptions.
It is about living amidst the *pain* and *suffering*
of this earthly life ..."

I still don't know whose words those were,
or if they were enough
to save my position in this parish
from those who would spread rumors about me.

Ran Loney

I slept, woke, moaned,
rolled back and forth,
bent myself in two with dry heaves.

I crawled to the creek and drank.
It all came out again.
I peed my pants in my sleep,
then lay in my pee, cold and wet.

One afternoon as the sky threatened rain,
I heard the sound of a vehicle.

A German tank.
It stopped beside the road.

"Okey-dokey, Loney, this really is it,"
                                        I whispered.

The door opened. Someone disembarked.
I closed my eyes and waited
            for the Jerries to find me.

I opened my eyes again,
poked my head out of my hideout.

The only human being I saw
was a small man — just
skin and bones he was —
clothing soiled, worn.
Striped pants, striped shirt.

He relieved himself in the grass,
then knelt down, drank in the creek.
            I walked toward him,
my arms clutching my abdomen
and was taken aback by his sunken cheeks,
his blackened hands, cracked
and peeling fingernails,
bare feet that didn't look human.

We stared at each other
            for some seconds, the way
deer stare at a hunter before flight.

Tried my French again — *Aviateur Canadien.*
The only gesture he made —
a nod of his head

toward the tank.

He walked back to the vehicle,
checked twice to see if I were coming.
He climbed in,
                    I after him.
He motioned for me to secure the door.

Slowly we made our way down the road.

He didn't speak any form of French
I could understand, nor English.

He drove into a village, straight
down Main Street, as it would be called
                              back home,
pulled into a petrol station,
tapped at the glass, the engine running.
We were filled. We kept on.

"Well, fuck a sad duck," I exclaimed, shaking my head.

George Loney

Holy shit. Never been inside
one of these contraptions before.

I floated in and out, checked
to see where this man was going.
I'da bet dimes to doughnuts he had a plan.

This guy was following the signs
to the French border.

We arrived at the checkpoints
in the middle of the night.
Coulda been daylight, all those lights blazing,
Jerry helmets all over the damned place.

The crossing bar lifted. We drove through.

Maggie won't believe it
when I tell her,
won't believe I had anything to do with it, either.

Margaret Loney

Jack Fletcher pounded up our steps
in his boots,
a telegram held lightly in his two hands
as though it were fragile,
as if something inside
were made of glass.

Nora opened it as the boys looked on.

C.P. Telegraphs
R.C.A.F. Casualties Officer
Royal Canadian Air Force
Ottawa, Ontario
March 23, 1942

Randall George Loney, Argue, Sk.,

Regret to advise International Red Cross quoting German information states your son Randall George Loney is believed to have lost his life January twenty-ninth but does not give any particulars. Pending further confirmation your son is to be considered missing believed killed. Please accept my sincere sympathy. Letter follows.

R.C.A.F. Casualties Officer

Addie Loney

I sat in Nora's lap.
Her face made my sweater wet.
Jim put his face
in his hands.

The stove went to sleep.
I could see my breath.

Carol Williams

That Agnes has true talent.

She waltzes in just when I need to concentrate,
says, "I simply don't know how Clara Innes
can hold her head up around town,
after her husband — imagine! A man of the cloth! —
has been seen with a scantily clad girl,
in the streets, no less!
I always did think
that girl was a fire waiting to get started,
and *he* is just too good-looking
to be a priest.

Louise says she thinks his nose is too long,
  but I don't.
And when something like this happens,
it always comes out that the girl
has been around the block,
if you know what I mean."

And then young Jim Loney comes in,
asking if there's been any mail,
and I always say no, like the cat
who just swallowed the canary.

I reckoned if they'd all just leave me alone
for one second, maybe I could fix it.
I went over to look again.
Shoulda steamed the envelope, not
torn into it, thinking
it was the Family Dependent Cheque again,
and it wasn't.

I always say, what they don't know can't hurt 'em.

R.C.A.F. Casualties Officer
Royal Canadian Air Force
Ottawa, Ontario
March 31, 1942

Dear Mr. Loney,

I regret to inform you that the Royal Canadian Air Force Casualties Officer Overseas advises me that a report has been received from the International Red Cross Society at Geneva, concerning your son, Flight Sergeant Randall George Loney, previously reported missing on Active Service.

The report quotes German information which states that your son lost his life on January 29th, 1942, but contains few particulars. The report does mention that the Stirling aircraft exploded in mid-air on the night of 29-30 January. Although your son's body has not been located, it is assumed he was killed either when the aircraft exploded, or in the event that your son escaped the aircraft, his parachute may have failed to open.

The International Red Cross is making every effort to obtain and identify your son's body; however, in the absence of additional information, his death will be presumed after a lapse of six months from the date he was reported missing.

May I assure you and Mrs. Loney of my deepest sympathy.

Yours Sincerely,
J. S. Johnson,
Squadron Leader, R.C.A.F. Casualties Officer,
for Chief of the Air Staff

Susanna Payne

I pick up the *Herald* every day
here at the boarding house,
a short walk to my college.
I have begun to make the trip there
and conduct my school day completely
without crutches.
I am heady with my new freedom.

But the *Herald*. I make a bee line
for the list of missing airmen, and pray —
even though my physician father
would never condone such voodoo —
that I will not find Ran Loney's name therein.

I made a bargain with heaven
that as long as I faithfully checked the listing,
my Randall would be well.

But one day, Mrs. Thorogood threw out the paper
before I had a chance to check it.
Three days later, my Ran's picture
appeared, sweet-faced and handsome,
quietly obedient within its frame,
            under the heading,
Missing — Presumed Killed.

And I now believe God
has punished me for my neglect.

Ran Loney

We lumbered through the French countryside,
stopped for petrol when we had to.

The hours passed slowly.
At times I retched, doubled over,
                but threw up nothing.

A night, and a day, and into another night,
and he turned, finally, into a lane. It was then
I realized he'd known exactly where he was going.
A building loomed in darkness.

He drove behind the house and stopped.
Someone peered from behind a curtain
on an upper floor. Only a thin line of light
escaped through the window.

Lifting the latch on his door, he motioned to me
to do the same. As we walked across the dirt
and neared the narrow back door,
someone descended the stairs
with a lantern. Light wavered
in the cracks around the door.
The door opened slightly, weak light
spilling onto the ground.

My driver whispered, *"Soeur Marie,*
c'est moi, Henri. C'est Henri, l'artiste."

A nun in habit raised the lantern to his face,
studied it for a time, gasped,
clapped her hand over her mouth.

The two stared at me. I began to speak
the two French words I knew best:
Aviateur Canadien —
but I was light-headed, and the floor
rose suddenly to meet me.

VII

Spring

Nora Loney

I think it's safe to say I have no talent
for the piano. But Jim, now —
never in my wildest dreams
did I think he'd take to music
the way he has done.

During the week he hums the piece
Mrs. Innes has given him to play.
He works out the fingering at his desk at school
and happily trots over to his lesson,
where his fingers practically dance
                    across the keys.

Granted, there is always food
that holds us through the evening.
But I've seen the way he looks at her —
as though she could make the sun
                    rise and set
just by smiling sweetly at it.

George Loney

Gawdam, what a place!
I've been sliding down these halls,
up and down stairs, get lost every time.
            But found the chapel

and sprinkled holy water all over myself.

Then I come to find out I'm not the only ghost here.
There's three, four —
sit in the kitchen at night,
shoot the breeze.

I tried to let Maggie know our boy's safe,
but what does she say to me but, "George,
now you get right back there this instant!
When you're not with him
anything can happen, and usually does."

I looked around our house,
barely recognized it.
Frozen, is what it was. Doors gone,
no furniture to speak of.

I said to Maggie, "What the hell..."
and all she said was,
"Burned."

Ran Loney

It was either sunrise or sunset.
I lay in a very small room
on an iron bed, squeaky springs,
a crucifix hanging on the wall.
I thought, *I hope that's not*
what they do to their guests,
turned over and fell asleep again.

A nun came in carrying a lantern
and a tray of food. I ate the bread
and melted cheese soaked in broth,
a few slivers of onion,
and drank most of the bottle of red wine
before sleep overtook me again.

When I woke again, sun stung my eyes.
I reckoned I'd slept a day or two.
A nun brought me bread
soaked in warm milk,
and sat like a heap of bed sheets while I ate.
Before I could drain the last drop
she rose, snatched up the bowl
and waved at me to follow her
to a large cold room,
a clawfoot tub
filled with heated water.

I scrubbed myself and lay in the tub
humming every old song I could think of,
until the water lost every ounce of its warmth.
Only then did I emerge.

New clothes lay folded on my bed.
Used, but in good shape. Shoes, too.
Where did they come from
and whose were they?
Short in the sleeves and the shoes
about two sizes too big,
but I could make do. I dressed,
and then, for the first time
on my own,
opened the door of my room

and wandered the halls, silence
buzzing my ears.
Suddenly, a nun appeared around a corner,
nearly colliding with me,
looked me up and down to see
if I were still among the living,
then motioned me to follow her.

We descended several flights of stairs,
traversed another long hallway
where she gestured toward the paintings on the wall.
"Henri," she said over and over.
"Henri."

She led me out the door and, checking
in all directions, crossed the lane
toward the great stone barn.
Knocked on the wide door.
It lurched open the merest crack,
and then
barely wide enough for me to enter.

My eyes adjusted to the semi-dark
just in time to see that I stood on a precipice,
the edge of an enormous hole.
The Jerry tank sat at the other end of the barn
like some bizarre, sleeping beast.

I recognized Henri among three others I didn't know.
All held shovels in their hands.
I looked into the hole but could not make out
who stood there.

Suddenly, it spoke.
"Well, fuck a sad duck if you don't look

like death warmed over!"

I knew the voice.
"Bill Harries, you sonofabitch!
What the hell are you doing here?"

"Never mind the formalities.
Now get your ass down here and start digging."

My eyes had fully adjusted.
That was the face of my pilot.
No doubt about it.

Jim Loney

Gophers are popping up out of the ground,
and at school all the boys go chasing after them
'cause they know they can get a penny a tail.

Frank caught himself a baby gopher. Now
he stops by our house every morning
so we can walk to school together,
me with our aircraft in the cigar box,
and him with his gopher, Roosevelt,
climbing inside one sleeve and down the other.

The girls crowded around to see that baby gopher
with its inky eyes, while Frank fed it grain
from his pockets and bragged how his brother
is in a German POW camp, how they're expecting
a letter any day now.

Between telling Nora how swell it was

she was back in school, Miss Parker said
Frank had to keep that gopher
"under wraps."

The whole schoolroom could hear that gopher
scratching at the walls of Frank's desk.

Ran Loney

We buried the tank.
It took the day and the night.
Henri, I found out, was rounded up
by the Jerries when they marched into France,
taken away to some prison camp
and climbed into the tank
while in the camp, as some Jerry
had gone off and left it running.
Drove right out the gates and down the road.

It was only right that Henri do the honors.
Shuffling uncomfortably in mis-sized boots,
he climbed into it for the final spin,
and drove the beast into its grave.

Bill took it upon himself
to administer last rites,
as only a former choirboy could do.
"Ashes to ashes, dust to dust," he intoned,
and made the sign of the cross over the deceased.
We then shoveled dirt into the hole
in unison,
with exaggerated formality.

The nuns came, witnessed the hole filled and tamped,
sighed with relief,
          crossed themselves and left.

Bill Harries, Pilot

After we gave the old rattletrap a decent burial,
Ran and I sallied inside and snatched up
a bottle or two of Bordeaux.

I wanted to know his story;
he wanted to know mine.

When I gave the order to bail out,
Nigel and I tried several times
to crank open Jake's turret,
                    without success,
the kite rocking and lurching violently.
We could see Jake, his mouth wide, yelling at us,
though we could hear nothing he said
over the din. Yelling, waving us away.

I grabbed my chute,
          turned and saluted him.
He'd pulled out the photo of his girl,
held it to his lips.

We bailed. Above our heads
                              the kite exploded
and lit the sky like daylight.
When I hit ground
          I counted five of us.
Ran was nowhere in sight.

A trio of Jerries leveled their bayonets
at us blokes not lucky enough
to swing like a monkey up in a tree.

"For you the war is over — "
their only words to us
as we were marched to a train stop
with others who'd been rounded up that night.

We crowded into an old passenger train
with bench seats
and luggage racks over our heads.
The window straps nailed down
to prevent us opening the windows.

While the steam engine took on water,
we painstakingly pulled the nails out
and carefully opened the windows.
We agreed that once we began pulling away
from the station,
we were to yell, *"Bon voyage!"*
and bail out.

The train pulled away.
The call rang through the car.
Howard Selemka and I bailed.

We hit the siding and rolled
down an embankment into a shrub.

Suddenly the train squealed to a halt.
Searchlights everywhere —
Jerries everywhere,
shouting and shooting in all directions.

We ran away into the night, swinging and swaying,
and didn't quit running until dawn,
when we found a low place
beneath some trees and dead branches.

A fortnight we evaded across Germany,
hopelessly short on food,
hoping to find our way to France.

While crossing a river, Howard was captured.
I waited in the brush, and when
the Jerries pulled him out of the river,

Howard met my eyes, and I knew
it was a signal to remain hidden,
but I couldn't allow him to be taken alone.
I moved to come out of my hiding place.

Just then Howard threw himself
against one of his captors
and fell on top of him.
The other soldier pummeled Howard in the head
with the butt of his rifle.
They pulled him up bleeding, half-conscious,
and between them dragged him out of sight.

Jake and Howard haunt me.
Scarcely an hour goes by
that I don't see of one of them in my mind —
the great, dark hole of Jake's mouth,
or Howard's eyes across the river,
Howard who left me, strapping and whole,
beside the water.

Nora Loney

Mrs. Innes declared we were to have
a music recital —
Jim and Addie and I.

Her house smelled like spice cakes
and apple cider when we came in,
shaking rain off of us like birds.

Adam grabbed Addie's arm
and chattered at him like a magpie.

And of course I played pitifully.
Jim played three pieces
and made it sound like real music,
left and right hands coordinated,
and seemed to relish the sound
nearly as much as Mrs. Innes's praise.

Then she brought Addie up.
He stood facing us, Mrs. Innes
at the piano.

She began to play, softly as she could.

Addie opened his mouth.
The words, barely audible, came forth,
clear and in tune:

Speed, bonnie boat, like a bird on a wing,
Onward! the sailors cry;
Carry the lad that's born to be king,
Over the sea to Skye ...

I felt as though the air
had broken into a thousand
prisms of light.
I wanted Mrs. Innes never to stop playing,
Addie never to stop singing.

Jim Loney

We walked home from our recital
Saturday afternoon,
the rain stopped for the time being,
the sun burst out from behind a cloud
like it was about to make an announcement.

The whole town looked rinsed and clean.

But we could see from a distance
a car parked in front of our house.

I opened the door.
Effie stormed toward us,
her arm straight out
and her hand spread out wide like a skillet.

Nora Loney

We moved the bed back upstairs.
Elijah drove his car three blocks to the depot
and brought back some coal. Jim
made a fire in the furnace hopper,
but the cold had burrowed

into the walls and floors
as though it were a sleeping animal,
and the house remained cold.

Effie bought groceries.
I made the supper while Effie
paced heavily through the house,
saying the same things over and over again.

"What in the name of Lucifer
have you ingrates done to this house?
I knew you couldn't be trusted.
Irresponsible, insolent little urchins."
Elijah Small stood around watching her
go from room to room.

"What if the Lord Jesus Christ
comes back this very day?
What will He do to me if He comes back
and sees the *Holy Bible* on the floor?
So this is the disdain you have for me.
So this is the way you treat my property."

She tried the radio. "How in the name
of Heaven and Earth am I going to listen
to *Gospel Hour*?"
Then Jim explained, exercising a patience
beyond his years,
that the power was turned off.

"So you little heathen didn't bother
to pay the bills.
That's what you're telling me."

Jim Loney

Effie dragged us to church.
Nora vowed never to set foot
in Reverend Meany's house
                    or in his church,
but she had to,
and sat in the pew with her arms
          folded across her chest.

Lots of folks rushed up to Effie,
welcomed her back
                    and didn't look at us.

After the sermon, Reverend Meany
called Effie and Elijah to the front.
They stood on the red carpet steps

and told how they'd gone to be missionaries
in California, how they'd come home
to find their house destroyed — no doors,
                              or furniture, or laying hens,
the Holy Bible lying on the floor.

The church took up an offering
for Effie and Elijah,
to help them start their lives over.

Nora Loney

After church, Effie stood beside the gramophone
and called us to stand in front of her
          with Reverend and Mrs. Meany present,

looking silently down on us.

Effie said, "You are no longer
welcome in my home."
She asked Reverend Meany to offer a prayer.

"Almighty God," he began.
And I felt as though he had placed
his cold, heavy hand on me:

"Almighty God, Father of our Lord Jesus Christ,
Maker of all things, Judge of all men,
we beseech Thee as thou hast promised
in Thy most inerrant word, that at the given time
Thou wilt separate the sheep from the goats,
whose manifold sins and wickedness
against Thy divine majesty hath provoked
most justly Thy wrath and indignation
against them. Separate them now,
that Thy obedient sheep
may hereafter serve and please you
in newness of life,
to the honor and glory of your name.
Amen."

We were to pack and leave immediately.

Dr. John Payne

Ruth Parker came to see me
in the lengthening evening.
We sat in the parlor, Mrs. Gabb serving tea.

It seems the Loney children arrived at her door
with all their worldly possessions in tow.

Which wasn't much, after all.
Now, I've seen quite a lot in my years
living in Argue.

I've seen babies I delivered with my own hands
grow up, go off to war
and come home in a casket or not at all.

I've seen a teacher run out of town
for speaking truths
which some people would rather not hear.

I've heard rumors abound
over a fine man, a family man, a priest,
all because of an act of compassion.

And I've seen my Susanna
shed her braces and walk.

I may leave this town some day
to live closer to Susanna.
Times are changing.
The small town, the prairie town,
may one day turn to dust.

I told Miss Parker
that I would contribute the sum of money
she'd come to ask me for,
and in addition I would pay
young Nora's Normal School fees,
complete, through to her graduation.

My only requirement is that
the name of the donor
            remain anonymous.

She seemed pleased. Speechless, truth be told.
Truth is, I don't want to leave this world
                        having simply taken from it.

I don't want, at the time of my death,
to have given nothing beyond
that which was expected of me.

Margaret Loney

I watched my children
pack their meager possessions,
their few pieces of clothing
worn through with erosion,
a few more
            from the St. Vincent de Paul sack,
a cigar box of hand-hewn toys,
faded photographs, old letters,
the rose dress, my pearl necklace.
My opera records.

I followed them to the teacherage
where Ruth Parker took them in,
and at night bedded them down
beneath her kitchen table.

The next day she brought Father Innes over,
who arrived with his kind eyes and smile,
and bore in his hand a scrap of paper

with a name and an address,
and slipped a bit of money to Ruth.

He laid his warm hand on my Nora's shoulder
and her eyes brimmed with tears.

Esther dropped in, charged fifty cents
just as I knew she would,
but cut their hair
                    to acceptable standards,
and Ruth paid her discreetly.
Mr. Freeman brought bannock and roasted hare
and told stories into the night.

Then morning again, and noon,
and my children stood on the platform
waiting for the train
                    to Moose Jaw,
Ruth having purchased their passage,
having hugged them thoroughly,
and Clara, too, come to say goodbye,

and young Frank promising to write
as the two boys split up their airplanes,
                    the gopher popping out
from the neck of Frank's shirt,

and then the whistle silenced them all,
and we found our seats, and slowly at first,
then rapidly,
            left Argue behind.

Nora Loney

We watched Argue and our little house
grow smaller and smaller behind us,
the bare land, the sky, grow larger.
I thought of the kindness
of Miss Parker, the Inneses,
                                        of Freeman,
and my embarrassment
when I realized, at last, it was he
had left us the frozen rabbits, the cordwood
on our back porch.

Addie fell asleep in my lap, Jim
stared out the window as though
he'd never seen so much land or sky
in all his days,
and I let myself pretend
Ran was working the train, and he
would strut down the aisle
in my mind, slipping us peanuts
and root beer,
            and I cried, of course.

And I thought how Miss Parker
refused to tell me who had promised
to pay for my schooling,
and her confidence
I would pass my entrance exam,
how she asked, "How old are you, now?"
and I replied, "Almost fifteen."

She regarded me seriously,
said, "Tell them you're sixteen."

Ran Loney

Henri has taken to painting again.
The sisters brought out his brushes and tubes,
his palette and easel and — God knows how —
found him a canvas.
In a sunlit room, beside a window
where he could look out on the greening of spring
yet not be seen, he began to fill that canvas
using whatever colors would still squeeze
from their tubes,
the color returning to his face,
the flesh returning.

Just after dark a man arrived on a bicycle.
The sisters knew him,
part of *Le Réseau Comète*,
the Resistance.
We would be given false papers
and taken to St. Brieuc,
where a ship would return us to England.

Two nights later Bill and I
said our thank-yous and goodbyes.
Henri rushed downstairs.
He'd just uncovered half a tube of cadmium.
Who knew that yellow could make a guy so happy?

I laid my hands on his shoulders,
blinked back tears,
wished him well.
Said, "I'll never forget you, buddy,"
and knew it was the God's truth.

Then, with our Resistance man,
we set out into the night.

Gord Saunders, Airman

The Jerries transported Howard Selemka
here, to Stalag VII-A,
a filthy and blood-stained cloth about his head.

When they brought him into our barracks
I could see he was no longer fully in this world,
the injury having done something to his mind.

Over the weeks he wandered
about the compound,
counting the barbs on barbed-wire fences
and taking a fancy to high places —
the roof of our barracks, mostly.
One of us would find him up there
and bring him down before the guards
could spot him.

In early spring, when the trees all about us
had sprouted bright buds,
Howard set forth
in the direction of the watchtower.

No one noticed
until he stepped over the warning wire
a few yards from the main fence.

The guards shouted, "Halt! Halt!"
The POWs called out, *"Verrückt! Verrückt!"*
to remind them he was crazy —
the bloke was not right in the head.
We leaped up and down behind the wire,
waving our arms.
But Howard walked on.

There wasn't a thing we could do.
They shot him dead.

I don't know what the Red Cross told his family,
but I sure as hell hope
they didn't tell the whole truth.

Jim Loney

When we pulled into the Moose Jaw station,
I showed person after person
the address on the scrap of paper in my hand.
Finally a woman pointed us south,
across the river.

I wanted to ride the streetcar,
but Nora shook her head, said
it would cost us *fifteen cents*
for crying out loud, and made us walk
three quarters of an hour across town.

Automobiles and streetcars raced past us.
We passed more people and buildings
than forty-two Argues smushed up together.

We turned up a tree-lined street,
the branches barely budding,
wind knocking them back and forth.
We stopped at a brick house, three stories,
whapped the knocker three or four times.

A round woman came to the door. Before
we could introduce ourselves,
she exclaimed, "Oh! You've arrived!

Mildred Walker, Boarding House Owner

Andrew Innes now — he and Clara
met at my boarding house,
and I'm proud to say it was I
put the bug in his ear about Clara.

Well, when he called, it just so happened
I had a room —
not a large room, mind you,
but a room nevertheless,
big enough to squeeze in a cot
for the little one.
And I feel for those children,
losing their mother and father,
and now their brother — oh!

Well, I set the three of them up,
showed them the bathroom down the hall,
the table where meals are served
at seven, noon and five on the dot,
and wouldn't you know, not three days go by
before that little Addie comes home
with a fist full of weedy wildflowers —
for me —
I hugged that child tight, I did.

Ran Loney

Dear Nora, Jim, Addie and the blue Saskatchewan sky,

Well, I'm back where I started from, you might say,
on British soil at least, and, well,

this may come as a surprise to you,
but I'm not dead. Nope.
Not even a little bit.

I've had quite a time of it though, I can assure you,
but have come through and am looking forward
to putting on a bit of the weight
I left back there with the enemy.

Bill, the pilot of our now non-existent plane,
and I the navigator of such, have received our assignment.
We're to report to BCATP Moose Jaw,
flight training school — instructors.

I'm considering already how soon
I can catch a train to Argue.
I've tried to make my excitement contagious,
but Bill isn't taking the bait.
Not yet, anyway.
I've told him about the hot, dry summers,
the cold, dry winters; I've been whistling
the meadowlark's song.

I slapped him on the back, said,
"Buddy, you've never seen a sky so big!"
And Bill retorts, "So you're telling me
there's not a tree in sight."

Pluck us a couple of chickens each. Make that three.

Your Loving Brother,
Ran

Nora Loney

I enrolled Jim and Addie in school.
Jim was not pleased.
He thought somehow, at nearly thirteen,
he could go to work instead.
He did find himself a paper route,
and I appreciate the money he will earn.
Addie's teacher seems kind and sensitive,
and I am grateful.

I found work at Hudson's Bay Company,
Millinery Department.
I can earn money to pay Mrs. Walker.
I'll study and take my college entrance exam
and enter Normal School in the fall.

The first Saturday evening as I left the store
to walk across the bridge, over
the wide railyards,
I had to pick my way through the young women
lining the streets by the hundreds,
in their best dresses,
waiting for the men from the flight school
to be let loose
to do whatever it is they do
when matched up with a town girl.

I myself could never be so brazen as that.

Margaret Loney

I have settled, with the children,
into Mildred Walker's boarding house.
She has a gramophone
which she calls a *Victrola*,
and I am pleased. At first
she seemed a touch unnerved
when I put on "Nessun Dorma" from *Turandot*,
as passionate an aria as I ever heard
and always makes me feel as if my lungs,
if I still had them, were filled,
                    fresh, cold and stinging.

But Mildred seems to be taking it somewhat in stride,
and has taken also to combing the boys' hair
at the breakfast table,
making cookies with Addie,
mending their pitiful trousers best she can.

And then George swooped in with the news,
looking so strong, so present.
I caught a glimpse of that one dimple
on his left cheek
and saw in him the young man I first knew,
and felt a smile steal across my face.

I said, *George. George.*
                    And held my arms out.
And my George came to me, and we danced
as Jussi Björling's tenor voice
boomed those high notes,
and the orchestra, swelling, took over.

It was grand, I tell you. Just grand.

Nora Loney

It was a bustling day at Hudson's Bay,
but slow in Millinery.
Two young officers strode through.
It seemed as if they'd had a few beers
and, taking a sudden fancy to the women's hats,
began to try them on.

I heard the one with the accent say,
"By Jove, if you were a lady,
not even a hat would help that face of yours!"

I knew I would have to go over to chide them
and send them on their way.
I tried to look stern, keep the corners
of my mouth from turning up.

"Gentlemen ..." I began.
They both removed the hats
and began to apologize.

I screamed.
Women from other departments ran to my aid.
I heard one of the men say, "Oh, my God — Nora!"

Susanna Payne

It is not unusual for enlisted men in uniform
to be seen in the halls of Normal School,
but I assumed the lanky young man
with the broad cap in his hand
had arrived for another girl.

When I heard him say, "I'd recognize
those blonde waves anywhere,"
I turned around,
            clasped my hand over my mouth.

"Apparently there's been a rumor going around
            that I'd met my maker.
I hope I haven't inconvenienced anyone."

I did what I had regretted not doing
the last time I saw Ran Loney.
I threw my arms around him.

Nora Loney

Ran and his friend Bill helped me to a chair.

Suddenly I felt mightily embarrassed
to be seen in my mother's rose dress,
frayed and faded,
            and completely mortified
to have fainted right in the Millinery Department.

To top it off, the kind face of my brother's companion
slowly undid me the more he attended to me.

We took the streetcar home,
                        Ran asking me,
"Are you all right? Are you all right?"
and me nodding through my tears.
Ran met Jim and Addie at the door,
pulled two lemon drops from his pocket,
Mrs. Walker busting her buttons

with pleasure,
her tears and mine suddenly contagious.

But I felt so plain
in front of my handsome brother and his friend,
and he, Bill, kept staring at me.

I thought, I must at least go comb my hair.
I must look a fright.

Bill Harries

Randall, my boy,
you did tell me you had a sister.
You didn't tell me
she was bloody beautiful.

Epilogue

I knew then I would remember the day
as long as I lived, and I remember it now
clearly,
as if I looked in on us through a window.

Ran and Bill arranged to take us up in a plane.
Of course, I wanted to ride
in a Lanc, or a Spitfire,
something Frank and I had crudely fashioned,
so that I could make real my dream
of flying inside one of those stick planes.
But it was only a civilian plane,
one with adequate seating for all of us.

Poor Nora clenched the arms of her chair
with both pale-white hands
as we were jostled and hurtled down the runway.

But then Addie and I, and Nora, too,
could not take our eyes from the sight below us.

The buzz of propellers filling our ears,
I marveled at the sky, enormous and blue,
and us in the middle of it,
the land below
touched with the slightest, fiercest green,

and the horizon not straight
as you see standing on the ground,
but curved perceptibly.

Before I knew it, we were circling over Argue —
the train depot, the Mercantile, church steeples,

our school, our house.

"Frank, look up. It's me," I whispered,
and raised my palm to the glass.

Such a tiny island in a sea of land.
Yet the world found us there,
and drew us to herself.

Acknowledgments

I would like to express my gratitude to the surviving veterans of the Second World War, and to the relatives of those who sacrificed their lives in that war, who told their stories, collected letters, photographs and memories of that time, and published them so that we might learn of their hopes and aspirations, their struggles and griefs, their joys and unmitigated tragedies that still define for us what it means to be human and vulnerable on this earth. I would like to thank Stuart McLean for reading a letter on his CBC radio program, *The Vinyl Café*, from a man who told of his encounter with a concentration camp survivor now living in Canada, and the incredible story of his escape. I wish also to acknowledge Barry Broadfoot's many volumes of oral histories which are a national treasure and largely forgotten today.

I would like to thank the Canada Council for the Arts for supporting the creation of this novel, as well as Patsy Aldana, my publisher, and Shelley Tanaka, my editor, who lent their expertise in shaping the manuscript while allowing me to maintain the integrity of the work. I wish also to express my gratitude to Russell Thorburn, my first reader, who marked up the manuscript in different colors of ink with each pass; to the Waywords, and to my fellow poets in the Glenairly retreats; and with deepest gratitude I wish to thank Lorna Crozier, who believed in me even when I didn't believe in myself, and Patrick Lane, whose prompt caused me to allow these characters to be born on the page, and whose gentle encouragement has helped me to grow in ways I never thought possible.

About the Author

Pamela Porter was born in Albuquerque, New Mexico, and she lived in New Mexico, Texas, Louisiana, Washington and Montana before emigrating to Canada with her husband, the fourth generation of a farm family in southeastern Saskatchewan, the backdrop for much of Pamela's work. She is the author of three collections of poetry, and her poems have appeared in numerous journals across Canada and the US as well as being featured on Garrison Keillor's *The Writer's Almanac*. She is also the author of a number of children's books, including *Sky* and *Yellow Moon, Apple Moon* (illustrated by Matt James). Her first novel in verse, *The Crazy Man*, received the TD Canadian Children's Literature Award, the Canadian Library Association Book of the Year for Children Award, the Geoffrey Bilson Award for Historical Fiction for Young People and the Governor General's Award. It was also named a Jane Addams Children's Book Award Honor Book and won the Texas Institute of Letters, Friends of the Austin Public Library Award for Best Young Adult Book.

Pamela lives near Sidney, British Columbia, with her husband, children and a menagerie of rescued horses, dogs and cats.

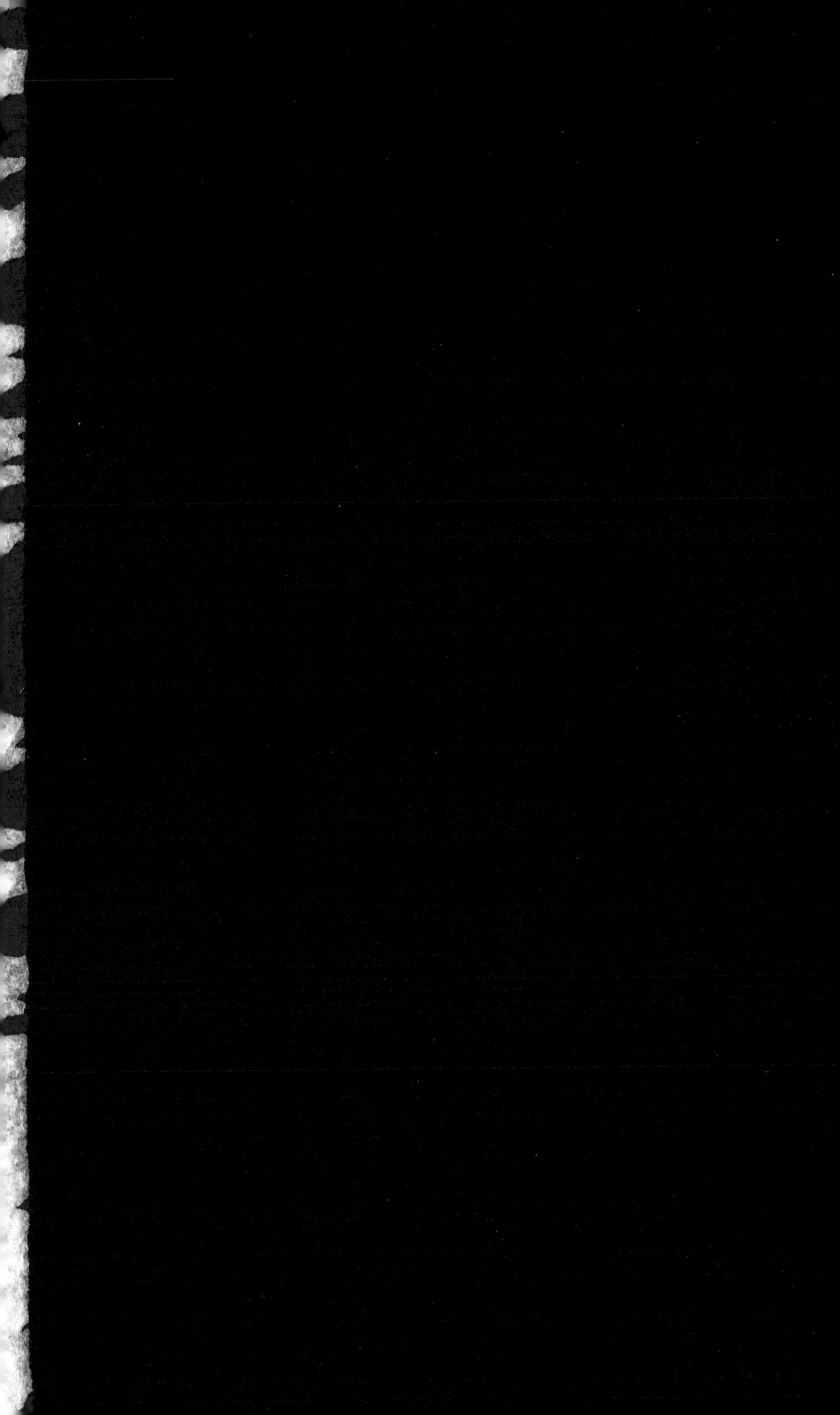

AR
RL
5.5
PTS
7.0